# Bolan is back!

*The Executioner is for real—ready to take on the world, to track down the human monsters wherever they may be, and blitz them out of existence!*

Bolan heard the sharp click in the dark. The sound of time having run out on a man's life.

But not on Mack Bolan's life. With a soft popping hiss, he squeezed off a round from his pet Beretta Brigadier.

A deadly Parabellum slug gave one surprised Arab terrorist the instant knowledge of whether eternity was filled with the beautiful *houris* promised by the *mullahs*.

Bolan ignored the shuddering corpse and moved on. Death was death, and the Executioner had seen too much of it to be curious about what a 9mm jacketed slug did to a human skull.

He had a job to do and there was no time to waste.

❋           ❋           ❋

This universe is a violent thing, created by a series of explosions. Bolan knows he is one of those powerful, explosive forces needed to maintain and sustain life itself.

His new war is a necessary war, a civilian defense of civilization. And, make no mistake, this war is the way by which Bolan will realize the potential of his own vast humanity. . . .

Death is merely the alternative to life. Bolan knows more about it than any living man.

# About the author

Don Pendleton is a much decorated veteran of World War II who saw action in the North Atlantic U-boat wars, the invasion of North Africa, and the assaults on Iwo Jima and Okinawa. He was also among the very first Americans to land in Japan just before the surrender, and he later served in Korea. He has since worked in the missile and aerospace industries.

An author of wide experience, he has captivated millions of readers with the compelling drive and absolute credibility of his writing. In ten years, Don Pendleton's *Executioner* series has become a bestseller in many languages throughout the world. In Mack Bolan, Pendleton has created a classic modern hero big enough to take on the most powerful forces of crime and terrorism.

"Mack is not a mindless killer," says the author. "He is proclaiming that humanity is important, that it does matter what happens here, that universal goals are being shaped on this cosmic cinder called earth. Bolan is an American hero whose actions are fast and effective. I only wish the world had more men like him, leaders with commitment, principles, dedication and bravery—the so-called old-fashioned virtues that were so evident in 1776."

Don Pendleton now lives in a small community near Los Angeles, where he continues to think and write about the man called Mack Bolan.

# MACK

THE EXECUTIONER 39

# BOLAN

## The New War

## DON PENDLETON

A GOLD EAGLE BOOK FROM
**WORLDWIDE**

TORONTO • LOS ANGELES • NEW YORK • LONDON • PARIS • SYDNEY

Published October 1981
First printing April 1981

Special thanks and acknowledgment to Saul Wernick for his
contributions to this work.

Man is condemned to be free; because once thrown
into the world, he is responsible for everything he does.
                                    —Jean-Paul Sartre


The American's conviction that he must be able
to look any man in the eye and tell him to go to hell
[is] the very essence of the free man's way of life.
                                    —Walter Lippmann


Fight not because you are told to fight but because you
are free to fight. Then you are answerable only to yourself—
and to the world you cherish most highly.
                                    —John Phoenix (Mack Bolan)
                                        from his journal

*Dedicated to*

Captain Richard Bakke, USAF
Sergeant John Davis Harvey, USMC
Corporal George N. Holmes, Jr., USMC
Sergeant Dewey L. Johnson, USMC
Captain Harold Lewis, USAF
Sergeant Joel C. Mayo, USAF
Captain Lynn D. McIntosh, USAF
Captain Charles M. McMillan, USAF

Eight brave American servicemen who
gave their lives in Iran during the
ill-fated attempt to free our 52 hostages.

We won't forget....

# CHAPTER ONE

MACK BOLAN SIGHED, lit a cigarette, stood up and gazed around at the mountain fortress he'd dubbed "Stony Man Farm." Yeah, the war would proceed from right here. Now. It would be a new war, a war against a new and different enemy. Although the face of the enemy may change, at his core he remains the same.

That enemy is Animal Man, whoever and wherever he is. Our goal must be to preserve the human spirit in all its goodness, and if a man has to die in an attempt to crush this savagery in whatever its guise, then so be it. It will, at least, have been a worthwhile war.

Does it sound pretentious for a man to aim so high and take on so much? Maybe. But unless a man aims higher than he thinks he can reach, he'll never know how high he might have gone or how much he might have accomplished.

I expect nothing beyond this day. My blood can be spilled as easily as I have spilled the blood of others. Whatever I can accomplish each day is just that much more that wouldn't have been done if I hadn't been around to do it. Call it my contribution to my fellow man.

But this time I am not fighting alone. It seems strange to me—I will have to get used to the idea that there really are others who believe as intensely as I do—that a few who hold power in our government have seen fit to give me their secret aid.

The time has passed when we can afford to sit around and watch the world go to hell, engulfed by a fanaticism so destructive it could mean the end of goodness and right.

The crazed animals we call terrorists would like you to believe they are motivated by a higher purpose—religious fervor, patriotism, concern for the oppressed, the redressing of old wrongs done to colonial peoples.

Lies!

They are no more than common criminals, motivated by a madness for power, for self-aggrandizement.

Oh, yeah, they're clever. And they're ruthless. That's what makes them so dangerous. Dangerous in the same way a mad dog is dangerous, and like mad dogs they must be eliminated to protect the rest of the world.

Of course we are hampered and checked in every way officially possible—by our own government and by world opinion—yet it is clear that the time is here for someone like me to be enlisted in this cause. Someone like me who has already proven the effectiveness of taking direct, forceful, final action against individual perpetrators of crimes against the people of our country.

Now it is against an enemy who is not only our enemy but an enemy to all the free citizens of the world...an enemy of humanity!

I believe that the primary right of every person

in this world is not to be a victim. This right takes precedence over every other right anyone else has.... And this is the right I fight for.

Yes, it is a new war.

And, yes, it is a war that will be hard to win and the odds against winning it seem impossible, but it is a war that must be won whatever the odds....

# CHAPTER TWO

NOW BOLAN WAS IN ACTION AGAIN, high above the steaming mountain forests of South America. He scrutinized the scene from the copilot's seat of a big Navy chopper.

It was not the sort of mission that a savvy warrior would choose for himself—but then Mack Bolan had never really known the luxury of picking his own, not in the deeper sense. In Bolan's hard world, the mission had a way of choosing the man, not vice versa.

This one had come looking for the man.

The man responded, immediately, unquestioningly, because really there was no one else. And because the request had come down from the Oval Office itself.

That directive from on high was terse, yet fully explanatory: "Find Laconia. Rescue or terminate."

The problem, Bolan feared as he gazed into that impenetrable rain forest, lay in the first mission goal. To find Laconia was going to be one hell of a trick.

There were new riders of the Horses of the Apocalypse raging abroad—he knew that. Where once the Four Horsemen had been Famine, Pestilence, War and Death, they were now Fanaticism,

Revolution, Terror and the threat of a technological Holocaust.

Who were these new enemies? What did we know of them?

Small, radical, insanely fanatical, they flaunted their hatred toward the established political organizations mankind had strived over the centuries to bring into being so he could live in peace with his neighbor.

Fighting alongside him, of course—and thank God for it, thought Bolan—were some of the largest friends a man could have, men and women he had come to love like the family that was taken from him at the beginning of the first mile. People who believed as he did. Who believed that this world was not made *for* people, it was made *by* people. That while the responsibility for a good and true world lay in the hands of everyone, those who were strong had a greater responsibility to see that it remained a good and true world. The weak, unable to defend themselves, could not be allowed to become victims.

The heavy helicopter had lifted away from the carrier at two hours before dawn, hugging the waves of the Caribbean and transitting the Gulf of Urabá for a landfall just north of Acandí, on the Colombian coast near the border with Panama. At first light they were right on schedule and flying at treetop level along a narrow valley set into the east slope of the Serranía del Darién range on a heading due south into the interior of Colombia. Vertical cliffs rose up on each side of the twisting, tortuous course, at times narrowing the way to a mere hundred yards across and often requiring the big chopper to make abrupt 90-degree turns as it labored along the designated track.

Now and then Bolan could catch a glimpse of the jungle river that had cut this course through the mountains—so narrow now as to be virtually invisible beneath the covering rain forest. He had another of those peekaboo glimpses at a bend ahead as the radioman coolly reported, "I'm getting pulses on the designated frequency. Sounds like a homer."

Bolan's blue eyes locked briefly with those of the pilot as he immediately rose and went aft to prepare for his EVA. Moments later, they were hovering above the treetops, and the pilot was reporting to Bolan, "Here's your spot, Colonel. Far as I can take you."

The two crewman aft smiled nervously at each other and prepared for midair egress as the big man in jungle fatigues moved gracefully into the cargo section and began rigging for combat. "Good luck, sir," one of them wished through soundless lips as Bolan twisted himself into the drop line. The warrior responded with a flash of icy eyes and a taut smile. Then he was EVA and moving swiftly in controlled descent through the treetops.

The familiar odor of jungle rot rose up to greet him, the humid warmth embracing him in its living presence, and suddenly Mack Bolan was back in his own element, the jungle master returned to the survivalist environment that had spawned him, nurtured him, provided identification for his life and manhood.

The Executioner was home again.

The air had its own special thick moist stench. Life teemed in it. Trees and vines and brush exploded grotesquely huge, fighting for sunlight. Torrential rains soaked the ground. Palms, balsa, mahogany and eucalyptus soared out of sight, their trunks wrapped in thick strands of vine, the deep dark green splashed with the brilliant colors of wild orchids and jacaranda.

But mostly there was the smell of death in it. Trees and vines and small animals died, and the stink of their decay was palpable in the heavy humidity.

Bolan knew the jungle as the place where he had first learned about death and killing and about being on his own against a brutal and ruthless enemy.

Now he was on his own once again.

He would find Laconia somewhere in this savage wilderness. Then he would rescue the guy from whatever unhappy fate had descended upon him. Or he would terminate..."with extreme prejudice."

It was, yeah, going to be one of those damned missions from which the soul of a good man is repelled—but from which the heart of a strong man cannot turn away.

It was going to be business as usual for Mack Bolan.

# CHAPTER THREE

APRIL ROSE TURNED LUMINOUS EYES to the White House liaison, Hal Brognola. "He's down," she reported cheerlessly.

Brognola moved quickly to the printer to scan the message for himself. He read the brief report twice, then transferred an unlit cigar to the other side of his mouth as he growled, "Sounds ominous."

"Sounded that way from the start," April complained. "What other kind does he ever get?"

Brief sympathy flowed in Brognola's gaze before the chill mask of officiality shut it off. "Are the others all here?" he inquired quietly.

She nodded. "Except Grimaldi. He's due in tonight. The others are waiting in the War Room."

Smiling without humor, he said, "Then let's go talk of war."

She hesitated for a moment, eyeing the printer, then smiled apologetically at the man from Washington and moved reluctantly toward the door.

"He's going to be all right," Brognola assured her.

"Sure he is," April quietly replied.

A freeze-frame of these two, printed and published in a Hollywood magazine, would reveal no clue as to their unusual occupations. The girl was tall and striking—a photographer's model, perhaps, or an actress—beautiful in every meaning of the word. And without working at it. She had earned a doctorate in solid-state physics, held a position of high responsibility with the criminal enforcement division of the U.S. Justice Department, and lately had worked at Mack Bolan's side during the closing days of his personal war against the Mafia.

Brognola was the polished, urbane image of corporate America—the boardroom type, carefully groomed and manicured, a handsome man of middle age, whose greatest exertion probably took place on a handball court. Wrong again. Hal Brognola was a street-wise third-generation American who'd worked his way through law school, apprenticed himself to the U.S. government via the FBI academy and a tour of duty as a field agent, and later moved on to the more interesting stratospheres of the Justice Department's covert operations section and into the strike forces against organized crime. It was in this latter capacity that he first met Mack Bolan. The rest was history. Between these two—one operating with a foot in the White House, the other ranging the hellgrounds of the underworld with no official authority whatsoever—the underworld power centers had toppled like dominoes.

Bolan had been given carte blanche authority to recruit and select his own staff and to operate in his own unique way. Brognola's job was to see to it that the "carte blanche" was honored wherever the official influence of the U.S. government could be exerted.

Mack Bolan no longer existed, of course, in the official sense. He had been recreated in the government computers as one John Macklin Phoenix, Colonel, U.S.A., Retired. And the entire Phoenix Program was a covert operation, unrecorded in the official records and forever obscured by several levels of bureaucratic smoke screen. Only Stony Man Farm, the headquarters operation in the mountains west of Washington, was officially recorded as a government facility— but even that was listed as a CIA "Quiet House" and covered by strict security.

Spreading across 160 acres of federal preserve high in Virginia's Blue Ridges, this "farm" had in fact served as a CIA training center during the early days of the Cold War, and had been scrupulously maintained since by GSA administrators. All of the buildings were in excellent repair. There were quarters for a 200-man force, a gymnasium and theater, athletic fields, and communications facilities that were now being upgraded for ComSat capabilities and for direct computer ties to Washington. Yet it was, after all, simply a facility. The *people* were the key to this operation, and each had been handpicked by Bolan himself.

Carl Lyons had been the first to arrive that afternoon, when Bolan was already winging to a carrier in the Caribbean by Navy jet. Lyons was once an L.A. city cop. That's when, by fate, he first crossed paths with the blitzing warrior in black. Coincidentally, Lyons and Brognola had been working together in a "stop Bolan" police operation when both decided that they should be supporting the guy—covertly, at least—instead of trying to sandbag him. Lyons owed several of his lives to Mack Bolan. But the big guy did not call in "tabs." The summons to Stony Man Farm had taken the form of an invitation, not a directive. Lyon's response was characteristic of the relationship between the two: he came immediately without question.

Jack Grimaldi was soon to come. He was a Vietnam-era "fly-anything" pilot working for the mob when Bolan first stormed into his life and offered him a second crack at true manhood. Grimaldi thought about the offer for a full five seconds before leaping for it. It had been a hard life ever since—life was always hard in Mack Bolan's cold world—but there were no complaints to be heard from this former Mafia flyboy. He would fly Mack Bolan anywhere, for any reason, with no more invitation than the twitch of an eye.

"Pol" Blancanales and "Gadgets" Schwartz held the longevity honors with Bolan. They'd been with "the Sarge" in Vietnam as members of the crack penetration unit known as Able Team, back during the time when Bolan first began to be called the Executioner. And they'd come to his aid in those early grim days of his lonely struggle with the Mafia. Schwartz was an electronics genius with particular credentials in the areas of electronic snooping and countersnooping. Blancanales had been a pacification specialist in 'Nam, a brilliant administrator and wire-puller (from whence his nickname "Politician" or, for brevity, "Pol") as well as a formidable warrior. Lately Schwartz and Blancanales had formed a private company known as Able Systems, specialists in industrial counterespionage. They had been doing very well. But the free-enterprise spirit could not match the magnetic attraction of an invitation to join Mack Bolan's world permanently. They'd been at Stony Man since shortly before dawn.

Others also had responded with the same alacrity. Leo Turrin was there. His place in the new organization had been preordained. He had shared peril and impending doom with Bolan for so long, and so continuously, that it would be unthinkable that their lives would take diverging paths at this point. Besides, Bolan had very effectively destroyed Leo's viability as an undercover fed who also happened to be a mob chieftain— mainly because there were no more viable mob chieftains, not at the moment, anyway. Leo was now taking quiet honors as an "elder" mob statesman without territory. His life was divided into three layers: as semiretired Mafia boss, as a Washington lobbyist with "connections"—and, of course, as an officer in the Phoenix Program. The first two were mere cover for the latter. Leo Turrin, heart and soul, was inextricably enmeshed with the ongoing activities of Mack Bolan.

These were Mack Bolan's "Stony People." They were the best in the business. Together, and with the covert might of the U.S. government solidly behind them, they could become the most formidable national security force ever assembled anywhere.

Right now their leader was "down" in uncertain territory and under questionable circumstances.

April gave it to the group without preliminaries.

"Striker is somewhere in northern Colombia. He has located the base camp of the man called Laconia Corporation. But the man is not there, and the camp shows evidence of recent and violent assault. It seems our spy planes have picked up what looks like an armed encampment in the nearby mountain area, and Striker is investigating. He's released his transport, ordered it back to the carrier. He is now tracking, on foot." She coughed delicately. "It is all jungle terrain. The Navy will attempt a rendezvous at the drop point in exactly twenty-four hours. That's all we know for now."

The long silence that followed that little speech was broken by Leo Turrin. "What do you mean by 'attempt' a rendezvous?"

April glanced at Brognola. "Well, there's a tropical storm brewing down there, just off Panama."

"Frederick," Turrin growled.

April's heart was evidently in her throat. "Is that...? I hadn't heard that it was...."

"It is," Turrin said sourly. "Upgraded to hurricane status twenty minutes ago and boiling toward Nicaragua."

"Well, that's good," Brognola insisted. "Isn't it? That's away from—"

"We never really know, do we?" Turrin pointed out. "Especially in the formative stages. It could make several false starts before settling on a track. I don't like any part of this."

Blancanales chimed in, "Gadgets and I missed the briefing, I guess. Who is this guy Laconia

Corporation? What makes him so damned important?"

"It's a code name," Brognola told him. "He's a deep-cover agent, Mideast territory."

"The new hellgrounds," said Lyons quietly.

"Right," nodded the Politician. "But why Colombia? If his territory is the Middle East. . . ."

"Well, of course—" Brognola paused to light his cigar "—that's one reason why we are so interested in Laconia. His assignment is the Mideast."

"So why," Blancanales repeated, "is he in Colombia." It was not a question.

Nor was the rejoinder. "Why, indeed."

"Maybe the hellgrounds are on the move," said Lyons.

April said, "Well, wherever Striker is. . . ."

"The hellgrounds," said Blancanales, "cannot be far away."

Brognola interrupted. "Striker has been briefed in depth and shown the photos of the armed encampment. Now that he knows Laconia Corporation has been taken captive, he is acting on a certainty that some questions will be answered at that encampment. He is prepared to act immediately, and alone. That's all we know."

Leo Turrin rose from his chair, cast a cold gaze at Brognola, and said, "I'm going to put some wires out. I have contacts in Bogota. Panama, too."

"Good idea," Brognola agreed.

Lyons said casually, "I think I'll check with Jack. He'll be wanting to go. . . ."

Schwartz got to his feet with a tight smile for

April. "Include me on that, too," he suggested. "Pol and I may have an idea of our own."

Brognola protested feebly. "I'm not sure that Striker would approve of all this. He wanted you sent to begin the organizational—"

April said, interrupting the chief, "Nuts to that. It's time now for all good people to rally 'round."

"All the stony people," Turrin said, smiling thinly.

"Them, too," said the girl, with a hard look at Turrin.

"I'll get to work on the *good* people," Brognola said, grinning. "You stony people do your thing. I'll take care of the rest."

Indeed. It was what he'd been angling toward all along. Hell, he couldn't have *asked* those people to. . . .

Leo Turrin was reading his mind. He pulled his long-time friend aside and quietly remarked, "You didn't ask the Sarge to go, *did* you?"

"'Course not," Brognola replied stiffly. "I merely briefed him on the problem. It was his idea to go."

"So you don't ask us, either," Turrin growled.

Of course not. These were the Stony People. One did not need to ask.

# CHAPTER FOUR

BY THE TIME DARKNESS FELL, Bolan had got up out of the jungle into the high plateau country. For the first couple of hours, he had not headed directly for the enemy hardsite that had shown in the air recon photos. His path took him instead on a wide sweep of the terrain. Overhead, a faint moon helped him make his way slowly through the countryside. He was looking for the road that led to the enemy encampment. Common sense told him there had to be such a road; it was the only way they could have brought in their heavy equipment by truck.

He found it just before midnight. From then on, the going was fast. The big man was able to jog most of the way at a steady, ground-eating pace, his muscles limbering up as he ran.

In the hour before dawn, Bolan was crouched only a few yards from the main gate of the encampment, scanning it through powerful glasses.

He wore a loose-fitting green-and-brown camouflaged jungle suit. His black night-fighting clothes were rolled and stored in his pack. But the powerful .44 AutoMag pistol was slung in its holster from his right hip, suspended from a military web belt. Beneath his left armpit, the silenced Beretta Brigadier 9mm pistol was snug in its own sheath. Extra clips for both pistols were stashed in canvas pockets clipped to the military belt that circled his waist.

The Stoner lay on the ground beside him, along with his pack. Right now, Bolan wanted information, not a fight. That might come later. Might? Hell, he knew it would have to come, but not until a time of his own choosing.

What the big man needed to know was where Laconia was being held—that is, if he were still alive. And Bolan didn't want to alert the opposition in any way, shape, or form.

Lying prone on the ground and merging with the shadows, the big man twisted the focus on the powerful night glasses. He closed in on the main gate—and the sentry who patrolled the short section of the tall chain link fence surrounding the compound.

Here, at an altitude of almost a mile above sea level, the air was clean, and even the faint moonlight was enough to give him a clear view through the night glasses.

He shifted focus to the buildings behind the fence. There were two long, barracks-style buildings made of corrugated sheet metal. At right angles to them and slightly off to one side were two shacks. To the left was a concrete-block structure, low and squat, more square than rectangular. Even at this distance, Bolan's keen ears made out the constant whine of an electric generator.

Towering above the buildings, supported on the steel legs of its framework, was the dish-shaped silhouette of a huge radio antenna, slanted at an angle toward the sky. The antenna turned slowly.

The big man remained prone on the ground, his alert senses sending out human radar signals. Night sounds came to his ears. Insects made high-pitched chirps. Wind sighed through the trees. Leaves rustled against one another. A small animal scurried fearfully in the high grass in front of him and then was gone.

Everything normal.

Bolan rose to a crouch and moved out, a black wraith slithering across the open ground to the fence, leaving the Stoner and his backpack cached behind him.

Timing it so the sentry was at the farthest point of his patrol, Bolan slid alongside the wire chain links. From his belt pouch, he took out a miniaturized voltmeter. It took a second to fasten one alligator clip to the steel wires. He touched the other probe to the metal, watching the face of the dial.

Nothing. The needle didn't move. Okay, so the fence wasn't electrified.

He filed the information away in the back of his mind.

The sentry turned, walked his beat, coming close to Bolan. Then he turned laxly and began to pace back to the gate.

Bolan rose and, again in a crouch, moved quickly into the deep grass of the clearing surrounding the hardsite, to his backpack. He settled himself in.

In the east, the sky lightened. Dawn was only half an hour away.

TWO HUNDRED MILES southwest of Cuba, the center
of the tropical storm gathered strength. Gale
force winds whirled in a slow, huge circle, forming a gigantic spiral that covered hundreds of
miles of the Caribbean.

It had taken five days for the hurricane to form
enough to be given a name.

Hurricane Frederick.

Normally, a hurricane bred to the southeast of
Cuba swings up in an arc that takes it northward,
sometimes into the Gulf of Mexico and then on up
through Texas or Louisiana. Or, it will hit the
Florida coast or Georgia and travel up through
the Atlantic states.

Hurricane Frederick was a rogue.

Spawned by weeks of blazing sun, hundreds of
thousands of tons of sea water evaporated and
rose into the still, hot air, forming great gray
clouds that began to swirl about a center. Gentle
trade winds had instigated the slow movement. As
the cloud masses grew, they generated their own
strength. The hundreds of thousands of tons of
water condensed as rain and fell and were hurled
aloft again and fell and rose. And the gigantic,
terrible forces created their own incredible static
electricity.

By the time the storm became large enough to
be termed a hurricane, each flash of lightning
discharged tens of millions of volts of electricity,
and the storm clouds had become black and ugly.
Massed, purple-blue clouds roiled in a devil's
cauldron of destruction.

Even before it began to move out, Hurricane Frederick had become a vast, destructive force.

It drifted off the normal hurricane track, picking up intensity and force as it moved. Swirling and churning in an enormous helix over an area of thousands of square miles, the powerful storm swung southwest, smashing its way across the island of Jamaica before heading almost due south.

Toward Panama. Toward Colombia.

Toward Mack Bolan.

# CHAPTER FIVE

SOMETIMES THE PRESENT is so much like a past event that what's happening now seems to be a repeat of what happened before.

It was like that for Mack Bolan.

Once again, his fighting apparel was a green-and-brown jungle camouflage suit. Once more, he was lying in concealment in tall grass outside an enemy encampment—alone.

In 'Nam, he'd spent days at a time, scanning a native village with binoculars, watching the comings and goings of the villagers, seeing a pattern of life develop, alert to recognize a difference when a Cong leader appeared.

So it was now.

Snugged down behind a fallen log, the high-powered Bausch & Lomb 10x50s brought him right up to whatever he focused on.

If it mattered, he saw that the new sentry at the gate was a young kid with a bad case of acne. He was also a lousy soldier. His AK-47 showed signs of rust on the barrel.

As daylight grew, men appeared, coming from the barracks, stretching sleepily, and then heading for a water trough to wash. The second barracks building seemed to be a mess hall.

Bolan began counting the hardmen. In five

minutes of scanning, he totaled more than fifty of them. All but a few were young, barely out of their teens, certainly no more than in their early twenties.

By the time the sun was full up, Bolan had checked out each of the buildings he could see— especially the huge, dish-shaped antenna that towered over the camp. For some reason, the camouflage that Brognola had said covered it was gone. It stood stark and enormous in the middle of the hardsite, turning slowly, the dish at an angle to the ground. Two heavy cables snaked out of its base, running to a circuit breaker panel mounted on the outside wall of the concrete-block building.

On the far side of the antenna base was the gray-painted mass of a huge generator. Nearby was a large fuel tank. The generator was a diesel. There was no mistaking the distinct, diesel throbbing that came to his ears even at this distance.

Bolan examined the generator carefully. It was a big son of a bitch, all right, and it was turning out one hell of a lot of amp power. How much power did they need, he wondered, to have gone to the trouble of bringing in a generator that size?

And why?

Certainly not to light up the camp. Hell, all the electric bulbs in that camp could be lit by a portable unit.

Searchlights?

He scanned the hardsite again. Not a one.

To turn the radio antenna?

No, gearing would take care of that. And re-

ceiving antennas don't require enormous power.
Not to pick up and amplify radio signals. As long
as the antenna was big enough to pick up even the
faintest signal, only a few hundred watts of power
would be enough to amplify so it would blast your
ears off.

So the huge dish antenna revolving slowly, angled at the sky, wasn't just for receiving messages.

It had to be capable of sending, too.

Yeah, that was it!

It was tracking something up there, and the
cloud layer that had begun moving in didn't mean
a thing to it. It was following whatever was up
there, locked on tightly. Satellites, most likely. The
orbiting treasure chests of space, filled with information more valuable than gold.

The door to one of the smaller huts opened.
Bolan swung his lenses over onto it. The figure
that emerged was shouting angrily. The big man
was too far away for Bolan to make out the sounds
that came from the guy's mouth, but the powerful
glasses brought him up close enough to see spittle
spin off the guy's lips as he screamed at someone
inside.

The face in his field of view was one he knew.

He'd seen it on the briefing screen at Stony
Man Farm only hours before. A swarthy, almost
handsome face, now contorted with anger.

Khatib al Sulieman.

Bolan was tempted. All he had to do was lift the
Stoner to his shoulder, aim and squeeze the trigger.

Yeah, set the weapon on single shot. Bring the V

of the rear sight up so the blade of the front sight filled the notch, with the Arab's head resting on the flat of the front sight. . . and squeeze.

Not much. Four pounds of pressure would do the trick.

And then feel the quick kick of the recoil in his shoulder while he watched the guy's head explode like a ripe cantaloupe smashed by a hammer.

But, he reminded himself sharply, Khatib al Sulieman was not—*repeat* not—his primary target.

Laconia Corporation came first. He had to find and rescue the agent with the strange code name.

Bolan chafed under the restraint, but he controlled himself. The Stoner lay untouched at his side.

Khatib started to walk across the encampment. A second Arab—this one short and heavy-shouldered—came out of the hut and caught up with him. The two of them yelled at one another, and then they started walking again.

Bolan followed them with the powerful lenses.

They were joined en route by a third figure.

Bolan did a double take. He refocused the glasses to be sure he saw what he thought he saw.

Yeah, it was a girl, all right. Long dark hair, twisted into a loose braid, hung over one shoulder. She wore baggy fatigue pants, but Bolan could see she had long, smoothly striding legs. And not even the olive-drab shirt could conceal her full breasts, unconfined by a bra.

She'd been coming toward them at an angle when Bolan first picked her up, and he couldn't see her face. Now, as she turned her head to talk to them, he got a good look at her features. Olive complexion; dark, thick, curving eyebrows over deep dark-brown eyes that flashed as she spoke; a nose that was slightly large; and a wide, generous mouth. Add high cheekbones, and you had one hell of a beautiful female.

Bolan wondered what the hell a girl like this was doing with a murderous fanatic like Khatib al Sulieman.

There was grim determination on her face as she spoke to the two men.

She was angry about something. The three of them paused to exchange words, and then, still shouting, they headed for a shack on the far side of the compound.

Bolan followed them with the lenses until they disappeared inside.

Was that where Laconia was being held?

Bolan lowered the glasses.

Khatib was the number-one man, but if the other two argued with him, then they ranked pretty high up in the organization, or they'd just have knuckled under the minute Khatib began ranting.

So three big shots were in that shack right now.

He had to get a closer look.

Sliding back into the deeper brush, the veteran jungle fighter swung the backpack onto his shoulders and picked up the Stoner. He began a long encirclement of the hardsite, moving quickly and easily through the concealment of the scrub trees and tall grass, yet never very far from the enemy camp, his eyes taking in every detail and storing it away for future reference.

The Arab hardsite was on a small plateau just below the military crest of the mountain. Bolan's goal was to reach that military crest. From there, he could look down into the hardsite from a new perspective.

And who knew what weakness in their defenses he might be able to see?

# CHAPTER SIX

INSIDE THE HUT, the face of Khatib al Sulieman glowered angrily at the other three people in the room with him. His dark eyes probed the face of the man who had been in the shack when they entered.

"Has he said anything more, Fuad?" he demanded sharply.

Fuad shrugged his shoulders. "Nothing that is new, my brother. He is unconscious most of the time. I don't think he knows any more to tell us—"

"Think? I don't want to hear what you think!" The hawklike features suffused with rage. "I want to *know!*" He spun around.

"Ahmad!"

Ahmad was lounging against the far wall.

"Yes, Khatib?"

"Has the prisoner said anything to you?"

Ahmad's thick lips split in an evil grin. "Many things, Khatib."

He slid the blade of his knife out of its sheath on his hip and stroked the razor edge with a callused thumb. "But most were cries for mercy. And yet—"

"Yes?"

"He may know more. Let us give him another taste of—"

"No!"

It was the girl who spoke. The heads of the three men turned toward her.

"Soraya? You object?"

"Yes. I believe he has told us everything he knows. He was screaming in agony last night. He was out of his mind with pain. He would have told everything—"

"Not a man like that," Ahmad interrupted. "I have seen men like him before—"

"And I have seen him! All you want is the enjoyment of inflicting pain!"

Khatib remembered that Soraya was city-bred, born and raised in Beirut. And Ahmad was from the Tuareg. Only the Tuareg were more callously cruel than the Bedu. When they captured an enemy, the night's enjoyment came from the captive's screams as they tortured him. Crooning tuneless songs, they would keep the captive alive as long as possible, slowly working him over inch by inch with their knives, until he went insane long before he died.

Ahmad growled, "You are soft, my little sister. Where is the hardness in you that our cause demands?"

"I am as dedicated as you!" she flashed back. "But we are not animals!"

"Enough!" Khatib cut through the argument. "We're getting away from what is important. We must be certain he's told us everything he's learned about us. And how much he's been able to send back to his masters in Washington. We're too close to the end now to have anything disrupt our plans."

Ahmad was still surly as he said, "They only know of our existence. Who we are and what we are doing they still do not know, oh my brother. Nor that we have a base here."

"I can't believe that." Khatib was thoughtful. "He admitted he made reports to them every week. He was on his way here when we captured him. Do you expect me to believe he didn't tell them where he was going? Or why?"

Ahmad fell silent.

Fuad spoke up. "What do you suggest, Khatib? Another session with him?"

"Yes. And another after that, until we are certain he's told us everything!"

The girl began to protest. Khatib's hard eyes were on her. She stifled the sound, biting down hard on her lip with her teeth. Angrily, she walked across the room to the door.

"Where are you going?" Khatib demanded.

"Out!" she replied, and slammed the door behind her.

NESTLED IN THE ROCKS above the camp, Mack Bolan unslung the Bausch & Lombs and sighted in on the camp. From here, some 400 yards from the chain link fence that encircled the camp, he had a view of the opposite side of the hardsite.

Slowly, he scanned the camp. There were the two long barracks buildings. There were three or four smaller, galvanized iron huts. There was the concrete-block building that housed whatever the hell was in it.

And, sighting in so that he viewed the back of the building, he froze.

And swore.

Spread-eagled against the concrete blocks that made up the wall, each wrist and each ankle shackled to an eyebolt driven into the mortar, his head fallen forward onto his chest so Bolan couldn't see his face, was the exhausted, limp body of a man.

Laconia?

Damn right. Who else could it be? Who else would be chained in such a position? Who else would have his shirt in tatters and thick streaks of dried blood criss-crossing his chest in deep wounds?

Bolan swore again, a deep, hard anger raging inside him at the kind of savages who would torture a man like that.

Off to the left, with his peripheral vision, he caught sight of a door to one of the shacks opening, and someone stepping out to stride rapidly across the compound toward the water trough.

Bolan put the lenses on the guy. Only it wasn't a guy. . .it was the same girl he'd seen before when she came storming rapidly across the compound to join Khatib al Sulieman.

He watched her go to the trough, pick up a pannikin, and fill it at the water faucet.

Carefully, she turned back, carrying the shallow metal cup. Bolan followed her with the glasses as she came around to the back of the concrete-block building. For the briefest moment, she stood in front of the prisoner. Then, almost tenderly, she lifted his head and put the cup to his lips.

Bolan zeroed in on the upraised face of the man.

Laconia.

Yeah, there was no mistaking that face. He'd seen it larger than life on the screen at Stony Man Farm during Brognola's briefing.

Except that this face was drawn and gaunt. Pain was written all over it. It was the face of a man who'd gone through an indescribable hell and still survived. The face was bruised. His nose was broken. Deep gashes had been slashed along his cheeks. His eyes were wild and feverish.

Bolan saw Laconia stare in surprise at the girl. And then he was trying to gulp down the water like a parched beast.

Through the glasses, Bolan watched the girl hold him back, making him take small sips. And then she wet a handkerchief and began to wipe down his face.

What the hell was going on? It was obvious Laconia hadn't given away all his secrets—or he would be a dead man by now. Did the girl think she was going to get him to talk by acting like this?

The big guy shrugged. It didn't make any difference. He'd accomplished the first part of his mission: Find Laconia!

In his head, Bolan heard Brognola's last words to him: *"If you can't get him out, then terminate him."*

Information. Analysis. Decision.

*Information:* Laconia was shackled to steel eyebolts in the middle of the enemy hardsite.

*Information:* The hardsite was surrounded by a steel chain link fence, guarded by at least a dozen sentries around its perimeter.

*Information:* He'd personally counted more than fifty of the Arab terrorists. Those on duty carried

AK-47s, and he was damn sure they were aching for a chance to use them.

*Analysis:* It would be incredibly stupid to think that one guy could go up against odds like that. Not only to go up against them, but to infiltrate the hardsite, free Laconia, and carry the poor, wounded son of a bitch to safety.

Yeah, that's what it would be, all right. Stupidity. Or worse. And Mack Bolan had never been into stupidity.

Taking chances? Yeah, sure, he'd been doing that from the day in the distant past when he started his war against the Mafia. Incredible chances. Against odds that no one else would have dared.

But never stupid.

Every single time, he'd measured all the factors and found a weakness and then exploited that weakness in the enemy's defenses.

And yet, his orders were clear.

Once again, Bolan heard Brognola's voice in his mind: *"If you can't get him out, then terminate him."*

From the spot where he was hidden, some 400 yards from Laconia, it would be an easy shot—*if* he had the Weatherby Mark V. The telescopic sights mounted on that brute of a rifle would guarantee it.

But the Weatherby had been left behind. No one had thought he'd need it, least of all himself.

The Stoner wouldn't be accurate at that distance.

He needed to be closer. A lot closer.

The back of the concrete building was about 50 yards from the encircling fence.

He had to get down to within a hundred yards. Or even closer.

Slowly, the big guy slid out from behind the protection of the boulders in which he'd hidden himself during the recon.

On his stomach, in the infantry crawl he'd learned in his first days in basic training, Bolan made his way at an angle down the slope of the mountain.

There was time.

It was only nine-thirty in the morning.

# CHAPTER SEVEN

AT THAT SAME MOMENT, in Virginia, just west of Washington, D.C., a rented Pontiac sedan drew up at the entrance gate of Stony Man Farm. The gate, like the rest of the fence, seemed innocuous. The fence ran around the entire perimeter of the farm. From the gate, a gravel road disappeared around a bend behind a grove of tall beech trees.

But neither the gate nor the fence was as harmless as it looked. Photoelectric beams and radio sensor beams angled invisibly across each section. For example, small animals were noted and recorded by central computers back in the communications building. Their size and mass were analyzed, but no signal would be given. Nothing in nature would be harmed.

But for anything approximating the size or shape of a man or a machine, it was a different story. Silent alarms would sound. The fence would be electrified instantaneously; or, the invader would be noted and allowed to penetrate the outer rim of defenses until he was out of sight of the road. And there he would be stopped, permanently, or temporarily until captured.

The driver of the sedan made no attempt to get out of the vehicle. He waited, the car engine idling.

Quiet chimes sounded in all the buildings of the farm complex. In the communications alert room, the CRT video display came alive. White letters skittered across the green face of the display:

```
VEHIC ID...PONSED...OUR ID: NONE...
REPEAT...NONE...
PERS ID...JAGRIM...OUR ID: #301...
REPEAT...#301...
IDENT     POSITIVE...VERIFIED...NO
OTHER OCCUPANTS IN VEHICLE...
ENTRY CLEARANCE REQUESTED...
```

Gadgets Schwartz turned a puzzled frown toward April. "What the hell is Jack Grimaldi doing here already? He's still supposed to be in Arizona."

"How would I know?" the girl answered.

"I don't like the car not having an ID," Gadgets muttered.

"Query him and find out."

Gadgets leaned over and tapped the keys on the console. The display on the screen disappeared. Almost instantly, it was replaced:

```
CODE 25...CODE 25...A-OK...A-OK...
```

"It's a rental car," Gadgets said.

"Let him in."

Gadgets punched in the gate release code. The system acknowledged.

Half a mile away, at the entrance to the farm, the gates unlocked and swung open. Jack Grimaldi gunned the Pontiac's big engine. Rear tires screeched. Dirt spun up in a high rooster tail behind the heavy sedan as it went flying down the gravel road toward the main buildings of Stony Man Farm.

April and Schwartz watched its progress on the big color television monitor screens on the wall.

"He sure as hell is in one big hurry," Gadgets remarked.

The girl nodded. "He's ticked off," she said. "I better meet him out front and find out what's bugging him."

GRIMALDI SKIDDED the sedan around in a half-circle on the gravel of the drive in front of the main building, boiling out of the car as it skittered to a stop. He ran up the steps, reaching for the door handle, but the door was opened for him.

"Hello, Jack . . ."

He dug in his heels and glared down at the beautiful girl.

"What the hell's the goddamn idea?" he demanded. "How come I was left out in the cold?"

"Left out of what?" April's voice was calm. She refused to respond to his anger.

"Don't give me that, honey. You know what I'm talking about! The bossman's gone off on a mission. Some crap-ass Navy pilot flew him down to the Caribbean. Another wet-behind-the-ears flyboy dropped him off solo last night. And there's a chopper pickup laid on for tonight, right? So how come I'm left out?"

"There wasn't time," April replied. "Come on in and we'll lay it out for you."

Grimaldi followed her.

In the den he grunted a curt hello to Schwartz and gave a bare nod of his head to Blancanales. He flung himself into a chair.

"Okay, start talking."

"First, we were short of time."

"I was in Arizona, checking out an aircraft. It's only a couple of hours by jet. You could have waited."

"Hal said there was no time to lose. The Sarge was out of here forty-five minutes before Hal arrived. The Navy had already laid on planes and pilots even before Brognola came out to talk to the Sarge."

Grimaldi was only slightly mollified. Ever since the time he'd forsworn whatever small allegiance he'd had to the Mafia—for whom he'd flown as a courier pilot—to become Bolan's flyboy, he'd developed a respect for the man known as the nemesis of the Cosa Nostra. The respect had grown into admiration and finally a love for the hard-hitting, single-minded ex-sergeant who'd taken on the formidable task of destroying the Mafia wherever he found them.

Time and again since then, Grimaldi had demonstrated his loyalty to his new employer. Now he ranked along with Pol Blancanales and Gadgets Schwartz as one of the hard-core vets that Mack Bolan had come to depend on for support and back-up.

Just as Gadgets Schwartz was a natural genius when it came to electronic and surveillance devices, so Jack Grimaldi was a natural pilot. If it had wings, he could fly it better than anyone else.

If it had rotors instead of wings, so much the better.

Blancanales spoke up. "Have you talked to Hal?"

"Yeah. He met me at the airport when I flew in a little while ago. He briefed me on what's been going on."

"Then you know there's nothing you can do. You'll have to sit here and sweat it out with the rest of us," April said.

Grimaldi shook his head. "The hell I will! I'm going down there—"

"And do what?" the girl demanded. "Sit around on your duff down there instead of here?"

Grimaldi exploded.

"I'd be less than two hundred miles from him! Okay, so I'd just be on standby, but if anything happens, I'd be close enough to get to him!"

Helpless in the face of this outburst, April looked despairingly at Gadgets. She knew exactly how Grimaldi felt. Loving the big man as she did, she'd have given anything to be able to be down there at his side.

Blancanales cut in. He was not known as the Politician for nothing.

"Hey, Jack, what're we getting so hot about? Huh? Talk to Brognola. Let the big fed make the decision. Okay?"

Grimaldi hesitated. April put her hand on his arm.

"Please, Jack?" she implored.

He finally nodded his head, giving in.
"Where's a phone?" he asked.

TWO HOURS LATER a sleek F-4 Phantom lifted off the runway at Andrews Field, pointed its nose almost straight up, and streaked toward the heavens.

At altitude, the pilot trimmed the aircraft and set his course into the plane's sophisticated navigation system.

The dirty weather ahead would grow worse by the time he set down at Howard AFB on the Pacific side of the Canal Zone, but Jack Grimaldi was happy.

Sit on his duff at Stony Man Farm? No way, man, not for him! Not when he could be ready and waiting to lend assistance to the big man if the Sarge might need it!

Here was one eagle who was going to do more than just scream.

EVEN AS GRIMALDI flashed through the skies at better than Mach 1.5, a coded message went out from the Pentagon in a brief high-speed transmission aimed at an orbiting communications satellite, which relayed it to its destination.

In seconds, it was received on tape whipping past recording heads at a synchronized speed.

Minutes later, played back at a normal 7.5 ips, the message was decoded, slipped into an envelope, and on its way to the commanding officer of the Air Force base.

In clear text, the message read:

TO: C.O. HOWARD AFB. CANAL ZONE.

HIGHEST AUTHORITY GIVES ADVANCE APPROVAL ANY REQUEST FOR AID OR EQUIPMENT MADE BY STONY MAN AGENT NOW ENROUTE VIA NAVYJET YOUR COMMAND. MISSION TO PROVIDE SUPPORT TO STONY MAN ONE IN RESCUE ATTEMPT LACONIA CORPORATION. MAX COOPERATION REQUESTED. THIS MESSAGE YOUR AUTHORIZATION TO COMPLY.

The name on the order was that of a four-star general.

# CHAPTER EIGHT

ALL THAT MORNING the hurricane moved inexorably and powerfully south and slightly westward in a great, curving arc, twisting in tighter on itself because of the earth's revolution. As the core spiraled inward, the speed of the circular winds increased.

Hundreds of miles ahead of the storm center, winds began to reach the land mass of the narrow Isthmus of Panama. The cloud mass thickened. Rain began to fall—at first in a light drizzle that dampened the ground and darkened the daylight.

Close to the center of the storm, on the small islands and cays, wind velocities reached more than 150 miles an hour, screaming like a thousand infuriated banshees. Palm trees were ripped whole from the ground, their roots torn loose as if they had been imbedded in loose sand, and the heavy trunks were flung like matchsticks high into the air.

Where the wind and rain ripped across an island, nothing lived. There was only the insane howling of the driving gusts and the blind fury of the lashing rain.

The center of the enormous storm traveled south-southwest at a speed that would bring it smashing against the isthmus soon after dawn of the next morning. It was headed directly toward the mountain where Mack Bolan was now crouched hidden on the slope, only a few yards from the chain link fence surrounding the hardsite.

He was now less than 80 yards away from the limp figure of Laconia, who was spread-eagled against the wall of the concrete-block building.

Within easy killing range of the Stoner M63A1.

The orders were clear. They left Bolan with no alternative.

No one in Washington Wonderland—certainly not Hal Brognola—would expect him to make a kamikaze attack on the camp in a wild attempt to try to rescue the secret agent. So...

"...terminate him!"

The Stoner was in his hand. He lifted it to his shoulder and sighted in on the figure scarecrowed against the wall.

The girl was gone. Laconia had lapsed back into unconsciousness. He hung slackly from the shackles that held him to the eyebolts in the concrete blocks.

A finger on the trigger, a slight pull, and, yeah, Laconia would never know anything about the bullet that had come smashing into him to send him into a deeper, more permanent darkness than he was in now.

Hell, he might even be doing the guy a favor. God only knew what those bastard terrorists had done to him, or how much longer the guy would live even if he were rescued.

But the Executioner never touched the trigger.

From the first, Bolan had known he would not

terminate Laconia. Not, at least, until he'd made his best effort in an attempt to rescue the hapless agent.

So that changed things, didn't it?

The big man smiled grimly. Information. Analysis. Decision. Yeah. He'd followed the sequence.

But who the hell said the final decision had to be based on logic? There was something more important to Mack Bolan than logic in this kind of a decision. Something called a higher morality. A morality Mack Bolan lived by and, someday, probably would die for. A morality that said a man's life was a sacred thing, not to be taken from him lightly, especially if he fought on the same side you did, for the things you believed in.

Bolan lowered the Stoner. He slid backward in a crablike crawl, retreating to his left flank to come around the encampment and complete his recon of the hardsite.

He was aware of the grayness that had come into the daylight and knew it was because of the approaching hurricane that the Navy pilots had warned him about.

He wondered if it would hold off until he made his rescue attempt.

He wondered if Laconia could stay alive until then.

And then he pushed all extraneous thoughts from his mind and concentrated on learning as much as he could about the enemy hardsite as he circled it in a tight recon, pausing every once in a while to scan details through the 10x50s.

# CHAPTER NINE

OKAY. Laconia had to be rescued.

And that meant Bolan had to set up an escape route from the hardsite to the point where the forthcoming rendezvous with the Navy chopper had been set up for the next morning.

And an alternate escape route in case that one wasn't feasible, because you never left yourself in a situation where you had no choices.

It was ten-thirty when he eased himself back into the brush and away from the plateau where the Arabs had set up their hardsite. He spent the rest of the morning and all afternoon making wide-sweeping recons of the terrain surrounding the plateau.

Just before dusk, not more than half a mile from the rendezvous point, he found a small clearing. At the far end was a thatch-roofed structure in a state of disrepair. Cautiously, Bolan circled it, finding several trails leading to it from a number of compass points.

Vines had overgrown the trails. None of them had been used in months. To one side of the shack there was a pile of charred logs.

Stoner in hand and at the ready, Bolan came up on the place.

It was empty. Inside, it was gloomy. Spider webs hung from the thatch.

A charcoal burner's shack. And whoever he was, he hadn't been around in weeks.

Bolan smiled to himself. It would do. Bolan's field headquarters. Well, he'd had worse in 'Nam. At the very least, it would keep him out of the light drizzle that had begun to fall from the thickening clouds overhead.

He looked at his wristwatch. Seven-thirty. The day had gone quickly, but it hadn't been wasted. From the gravel road bulldozed along the steep slope of the mountain for two miles around the enemy hardsite, the big guy knew the terrain intimately.

He wondered if the enemy knew it as well as he did.

KHATIB AL SULIEMAN WAS ALONE in the hut that served him for both an office and living quarters. He slept on a narrow cot in one corner of the shack. Three planks on sawhorses served him as a desk.

Ahmad and Fuad were in the concrete-block building, programming the final details into the big computers.

And Allah alone knew where Soraya was, Khatib thought. Something had got into the girl. She was not the same fiery-eyed, hot-tempered Lebanese he had known for the past two years. Something had changed. Ever since they'd captured that infidel American agent and Ahmad had gone to work on him . . .

With an oath, he thrust the thought of her out of

his mind. He had more important things to do on this day! Tomorrow would see the culmination of all their efforts, all their plans. And when it was over, the name of Khatib al Sulieman would resound throughout the Islamic world!

He smiled at the thought.

Khatib al Sulieman. Age 29. Born in the Gaza Strip to refugee Palestinian parents who later fled to Syria.

Oh, he remembered the years, all right. He remembered growing up as a hungry child, being taught in small, stinking sheds that served as classrooms. Along with his lessons in learning to read and write Arabic, he learned to hate the Israelis.

He learned more than just what the gray-bearded *mullahs* taught him. He also learned to shoot a gun.

By the time he was ten, the *fedayeen* had taught him how to aim and fire a Kalashnikov AK-47 assault rifle and how to field-strip it and reassemble it in minutes.

At fourteen, he went on his first raid, sneaking down from the Golan Heights at night. There had been five of them, he remembered, but he was the only one to return. The *kibbutz-niks*, aroused, had killed the others. Only Khatib got away. He came back to brag about his three victims. The fact that two of them were children and the other an old woman, he kept to himself.

At sixteen, he'd planted plastique bombs in parked autos in Tel Aviv and Jerusalem. The death toll amounted to more than fifty before he was through. Unfortunately, twelve of them were Arabs.

But Khatib was also bright. At nineteen, he entered the university in Beirut. At twenty, he won a scholarship to the London School of Economics. Graduated with honors at twenty-three, he did not go back to Syria. He dropped out of sight. The leadership of the PLO was too conservative for him.

His anger, burning deep inside him, needed greater violence than they could provide.

Mossad, the Israeli counterpart to the CIA, had sightings of him in Germany. He had been linked to the Baader-Meinhof Gruppe.

Other sightings involved him with the Red Brigade in kidnappings in Italy.

Always talk about him. Always rumors. And always about his cleverness and brilliance.

And then he dropped completely out of sight.

That was when he had met up with Soraya. Soraya Naseer.

By Allah, she was something! Not for her the feminine clothing many Lebanese women wore! Nor the drab clothing Syrian women wore to conceal their bodies from the lewd glances of men.

No! Soraya dressed like a man, acted like a man, her mind filled with a hatred as great as his own.

And she gave herself like no woman he'd ever had in his life. The Arab knew he was fortunate she had chosen him for her lover.

It had been Soraya who'd talked him into this undertaking. Yes, it had been his idea, but he hadn't seen its full import until the girl pointed it out to him.

It had been his creation, but it was Soraya, her eyes burning with revolutionary fervor, who'd shown him that if he carried it out, the Hawks of the Revolution would no longer be a minor splinter group.

They'd have millions in their treasury to back them up. No longer would they have to depend on handouts from one or the other of the Arab sheikh-doms, or from that fanatical Libyan, Khaddafi.

Together, the two of them had recruited the men they needed. Together, they had found Ahmad Mashir and Fuad al Shawwa.

Ahmad. Desert born, he was as bloodthirsty as any of his tribal ancestors. And yet Ahmad was a graduate of Cambridge University with degrees in engineering and a Ph.D. from M.I.T.

Fuad al Shawwa. A heavyset young man with a pockmarked face, who looked like a slum cut-throat. A hard man if there ever was one. But Fuad was a graduate of Stanford University with degrees in electronic engineering and computer science. It was Fuad who'd come up with the designs for the equipment that had been erected on the concrete base outside and whose bowl-shaped antenna was focused on a U.S. satellite, tracking to a fraction of a degree the orbit it followed.

Tomorrow it would be in position.

And by tomorrow, it would be pirating informa-tion, secret and highly significant information, that could change the balance of power in the world overnight.

As soon as Khatib could bleed that satellite of its facts and figures, he would turn his five deadly missiles on a target so perfect it was laughable! Then America, with all its wealth and technology and spaceware, would be begging!

Begging Allah for mercy! And for oil: for enough oil to get by one day at a time....

# CHAPTER TEN

ALL AFTERNOON the storm front had moved closer. Overhead, the cloud mass thickened. The heavy mist was still little more than a drizzle, but everything was damp. And the wind began to rise, stirring the wet leaves.

Nine o'clock. Time for the big man to move out. Time once more for Mack Bolan to put his life on the line to get another job done.

Yeah, it could have been done without risk—if he'd taken the option to terminate Laconia. But he had deliberately, instinctively, chosen to rescue the agent. And so the situation had come down to this. One man going into hell one more time—to pit his skill and ability against overwhelming odds, to challenge a vicious, ruthless enemy.

A thought crossed Bolan's mind, causing him to smile grimly.

This new war—against a new enemy—it wasn't so different after all, was it?

BOLAN STEPPED OUT of the charcoal burner's hut, into the dark and the wet. He slung his pack onto his shoulders and fastened the straps for a tighter fit. The 5.56mm Stoner was in his right hand, balanced differently than usual because of the 150-round aluminum drum clipped into its receiver, but still a familiar and comforting weight.

He drew in a deep breath, looked down at his wrist compass, oriented himself, and stepped off, heading for the darker mass of the mountain peak a mile-and-a-half away, lighting his way from time to time with faint luminescence from a red-lensed flashlight.

THREE-QUARTERS OF AN HOUR LATER, Mack Bolan was crouched outside the perimeter of the chain link fence, hidden this time by the darkness of night.

The big man was now in blacksuit. His face and hands were blackened. His feet were shod in black sneakers. The powerful .44 AutoMag pistol was slung in its holster on his right hip, suspended from the military web belt.

The silenced Beretta Brigadier 9mm pistol was snug in its sheath beneath his left armpit. Extra clips for both pistols were stashed in canvas pockets clipped to the web belt that circled his waist. Slit pockets in the legs of his blacksuit contained a variety of useful implements and accessories, including a deadly slim stiletto.

The backpack and the Stoner were cached some 50 yards behind him, at the base of a dead tree. This was to be a soft probe. Laconia had to be brought out before the terrorists became aware he was missing. There was no way Bolan could blitz his way into the hardsite, grab the secret agent, and fight his way out again.

Not without turning the hardsite into a hell-ground. A hellground in which neither he nor Laconia stood a chance of coming out alive.

Wiping the mist off the lenses of the binoculars, Bolan saw that the guard pattern was the same. But now the wind had risen and they were wet and the sentries walked their rounds carelessly, with their heads down.

Sentries? Hell, they were walking victims looking for someone to take them out one at a time.

But not now. Later, perhaps.

QUIETLY, THE DEADLY NIGHTFIGHTER circled the ground some 20 yards away from the fenced perimeter of the camp. Half an hour of silent movement brought him around to the back of the hardsite along the slope that led to the mountain's crest.

Bolan settled himself into position and brought the 10x50s to his eyes.

His target: the squat concrete-block structure and its back wall, against which he had seen Laconia spread-eagled that morning.

Slowly he scanned it, a frown growing on his forehead. His fingers turned the focusing knob of the glasses.

Goddamn it! The wall was bare!

Laconia was no longer shackled to it. Through the powerful lenses, Bolan sought and found the eyebolts in the mortar between the blocks.

But Laconia was gone!

When had he been moved?

A heavy feeling grew in the pit of Bolan's stomach. Had he loused up the mission? Had he allowed his personal feelings to enable the enemy to learn what they never should have got out of the secret agent?

Was Laconia still alive? Or had he been taken down because he was dead?

Bolan swore again.

He was back to square one.

*Find Laconia....*

He tucked the night glasses back into their case, which was slung from his web belt. He slid down the slope through the darkness to the chain link fence, again timing his arrival when the sentry was at the farthest point of his beat.

Lying prone on the ground, he took a pair of wire cutters from their holster at his waist. He had no hesitation in putting them to the steel. His morning's probe had shown him that the fence wasn't electrified.

In less than three minutes of work, he had snipped a gash in the chain link barricade high enough for him to slide through on his back.

And then he was inside, on his feet, a deadly black ghost drifting along like ground fog.

Bolan crossed the width of the area between the buildings and the fence, moving with swift determination, sacrificing a small amount of secrecy for speed.

Suddenly the glint of metal on the ground stopped his advance. He touched the cold, shining bars with his hands and realized they were rail tracks. Before proceeding further, he peered into the darkness on each side of him, trying to see where the rails led.

On his left, only yards away, loomed two strange shapes. They looked stranger still as his eyes focused in the darkness. Twenty feet tall at least.

The black towers against the night looked like deformed totems.

Bolin could smell the canvas now and realized what it was that made these things parked on the rails look so misshapen. The tarpaulin was camouflaging objects that he guessed were smooth and sleek and no mystery at all: surface-to-air ballistic missiles.

As he stared at them for just seconds more, he noted further shadows to their rear. His estimation right now was five or six of the deadly devices. And the odor of oil and nitrogen, mingling with the smell of all the other supplies here in the darkness, suggested the missiles were ready to spit fire at a second's notice. He guessed they were of the kiloton variety, and by the size of them had a probable range of 200 miles. What target was 200 miles from this godforsaken part of Colombia?

Bolan darted across to the nearest building. There was much more for him to probe in this strange place. He crouched down at a small window waist high in the wall. Carefully, he eased himself up.

A yellow glow came from the window, spilling in an oblong shape onto the wet ground. His face pressed against the rough cement of the blocks. And then a fast turn of his head, a momentary scan in through the window, and he turned his head away from it again.

Crouched at the base of the wall, his mind imprinted with what he had seen, Bolan tried to make sense out of it.

The room was crammed with computer equipment. Two walls were taken up with enormous banks of painted gray steel cabinets. There were two high-speed printers and two separate input consoles.

What the hell did it mean?

He had no time to finish his train of thought. His keen ears picked up the tread of someone rounding the corner of the shack.

The silenced Beretta greased its way into his hand from its holster under his left armpit. In the same motion, he flicked off the safety.

Bolan was ready and waiting when the hardguy stepped around the corner, yet he held his fire. Unless he had to, he preferred to make this probe without alerting anyone.

But it wasn't to be.

The guard had come around the corner, leaning into the wind, his head down. Suddenly he stopped. His head came up and swung left and then right, and the AK-47 assault rifle in his hands began to swing up.

Whatever instinct that had caused the sentry to realize he wasn't alone proved to be his undoing. Bolan heard the sharp click as the guy pulled off the safety on the AK-47.

Time had run out on a man's life.

But not on Bolan's life. He lifted the Beretta, squeezing off a round. There was a soft, popping hiss, and a deadly Parabellum slug let the Arab terrorist know the dark eternity he'd given to so many others. In that fraction of a second, the revolutionary tough guy found out whether or not Paradise was filled with *houris* as the *mullahs* had promised. But now he was in no shape to let anyone know what he'd learned...

Bolan leaped forward as the guy sagged. His quick hands caught the heavy assault rifle before it could hit the ground. The Arab hardguy lay in a death sprawl, face up.

Bolan knelt beside him. He didn't need to examine the guard to know that the small, round hole in his forehead would be matched by a huge cavity in the back of his head, where bone and brain matter had been torn away.

Death was death, and the Executioner had seen too much of it to be curious about what a 9mm jacketed slug did to a human skull. Quickly, Bolan pulled the body straight and rolled it against the wall, where it couldn't be spotted easily.

Now he had less time than before to find out where they were holding Laconia. Someone was going to be sure to look for a missing guard when his tour of duty was up.

Okay, then. Where would it be likely the secret agent was being held?

Certainly not in either of the barracks-type buildings. So it had to be in one of the several smaller galvanized-iron huts. Light came out of the windows of two of them. The third was dark.

Pick one of the lighted ones. Which? Bolan threw a fast eyeball around the compound clearing and then raced to the nearest.

Once more the careful slide up the wall to the window. Once more the slow turning of his head and the rapid glance inside.

And, once more, the face of the swarthy Arab

with the cruel features he had seen on the screen at the Stony Man Farm briefing!

Khatib al Sulieman.

The face was in profile. The Arab was bent over his makeshift desk, engrossed in writing.

Once more, chance had provided Bolan with an opportunity to rid the world of the Arab bossman. A squeeze of the Beretta trigger.

But again he had to forgo the execution.

He reminded himself that his mission was not to execute the saturnine, blood-hungry Arab. Finding Laconia—rescuing Laconia—came first.

Wonderland needed Laconia's information more than it needed the death of Khatib al Sulieman.

If he killed the Arab bossman now, the first person to come to Khatib's shack would sound the alarm and blow Bolan's chances of rescuing the agent.

By now Bolan wanted to know a great deal more about Khatib al Sulieman and his gang. Quite apart from wanting to destroy them all before it was too late.

What sort of terrorist gang was it that would make a full-fledged tactical base for itself in these mountains? That's what this place sure as hell looked like: a task-force base, equipped with a satellite tracking dish, massive computer systems, a generator big enough to light a small town.

The layout reminded Bolan of the blueprints and reconnaissance photographs he had seen of Intelsat communication stations, now prime targets in the space spy-probe race that had been escalating between the East and West in the 1970s and early '80s.

The team at Stony Man knew all about them; they were playing a major part in the big powers' arms stand-off, and Bolan's people had researched them well. But to find anything of the kind right here in the remotest of regions . . . and manned by terrorists answerable only to their own force of evil . . . it made the flesh creep.

With his distaste suppressed by a strong, urgent curiosity, Bolan crept along the side of the hut until he came to a gap where some tossed-aside construction materials were lying on the ground, and then to another small building. Farther along the wall of this other shack was a small, one-foot-by-one-foot window from which a weak light emerged.

He looked in. A single bulb cast a pale light across stacks of what appeared to be clothing, cardboard boxes, wooden crates, plastic-wrapped packages. This was a supply cache of some sort. Worth a closer look.

The door to the right of the window opened with a swift jimmy and a silent shoulder nudge. His probe of the hut and its contents confirmed Bolan's hunch. This scuba gear, the sonar equipment, inflatable dinghies—and a crate of eight limpet mines—were the latest in underwater demolition equipment.

Also visible were stacks of uniforms with Russian markings. But the men here obviously were not Communist terrorists; they were Arab independents with backing from a variety of sources. Nevertheless, the familiar Russian insignia on this dank-smelling wool clothing troubled Bolan deeply.

Damn, the base had to be the strangest place in all of South America at this point in time. What he had stumbled on in his search for Laconia was no mere terrorist hang-out. It was a time bomb. It was a deadly button waiting to be pushed. Bolan's profoundest instinct was to nullify it right now, to take immediate preventive action and wipe the place off the face of the earth before its variety of repulsive poisons were released on innocent populations.

Steady. There were plans to be made, plans to follow. He exited the supply shack and stealthily returned to the window of Khatib's building. From a slash pocket in the left leg of his blacksuit, he took out a microminiaturized limpet "bug." Gadgets had recently provided him with a number of his newest toys. No larger than a shirt button, with an adhesive backing, the bug could transmit for almost half a mile.

Bolan stuck it to the glass in the lower right-hand corner of the window. The whole pane would serve to amplify any sounds within the hut even before the bug itself picked up the sound.

Bolan slipped around the corner and turned away from the shack. Another quick eyeball of the compound. No sentries in sight. He raced for the second of the two lighted huts.

This time, the fast scan through the window revealed two men. One of them he'd seen earlier that day, walking with Khatib al Sulieman. The other was new to him. They were arguing with each other.

In less than a minute, Bolan planted another limpet bug on the glass of the window. An earphone went into his left ear, the subminiature plug on the end of a threadlike cord snapped into the tiny jack in the flat, cigarette-pack size receiver, and Bolan heard them talking—in Arabic!

The big man was amused at himself. Hell, what did he expect? That they'd be speaking English?

But the scan had also revealed that Laconia wasn't being held in this shack either.

So that left only the darkened hut.

Time was whipping by faster than he wanted it to. How much longer would it be before someone discovered the missing sentry and went looking for him?

For the third time, Mack Bolan scanned the deserted stretch of ground in the center of the hardsite. The darkened shack was on the far side. What he wanted to do was race across the space, taking a chance that no one would see him.

But it was a chance he didn't dare gamble on.

He made his way back to the concrete-block building. The dead body of the sentry was still there, undiscovered.

Bolan sighted in on the dark shack, now only a few yards away to his right.

A deep breath, and he was sprinting across the short distance, the sound of the wind covering up any footfall on the moist earth.

He pushed himself up alongside the galvanized iron sheets that made up the wall of the hut. The darkness inside prevented him from seeing anything.

But there was a way to find out. A third limpet bug went onto the window glass, and again the earphone went into his ear.

Bolan switched on the battery power.

Whispers... a soft voice crooning gently... a slight noise he recognized as the splash of water.

The voice grew louder, but it was still a whisper. And in English: "...hate them," said a girl's voice. "Never... I never thought it would be like this!... Lie still... I will wash your face...."

Bolan heard the splash of water again. It was the sound of a hand splashing in a basin.

A hoarse, tired voice answered her, also in a whisper.

"What did you think...." There was a soft gasp of pain, and then, "...did you think it would be like?"

"I don't know. My mind was filled with... ideas.... Revolution! That is the answer to... everything. Philosophy. Theory."

"But you knew you had to... to kill."

"Talk. It's so easy to talk. Oh, yes, I could talk about killing the dictators and the oppressors of my people. But until now... I was involved only in... in the plans.... Not in...."

"Torture?"

Laconia!

"What... they did... to you. I tried to shut my ears to it... but there are limits."

The girl was almost crying now.

"I didn't think... I would be... so soft!... I am ashamed of myself. I thought we were fighting against inhumanity... against people being tortured by the secret police... but we are no better than they... are we?"

Laconia gasped in pain.

The girl said sorrowfully, "I... wish... I could do more for you."

"You...you've done...a...lot. Thank you..." Laconia gasped out the words.

Mack Bolan had heard enough. Swiftly, he stepped around the corner of the building, and with one quick step, he was inside the open door of the darkened shack.

"If you want to do more," his voice whipped into the darkness, quietly but with steel in it, "you can help me get him away from here!"

A sudden intake of breath from the startled girl. Bolan snapped on his red-lensed flashlight, aiming it so a pale red glow suffused the hut.

He saw her eyes widen as she took in his black-clad figure, draped with armament. Her mouth opened to cry out.

"Don't make a sound," he warned. "Whisper, if you want to talk."

The girl stared incredulously at him, her oval face pale in the red light.

"Who...are you?"

Her eyes were fastened on the huge .44 Auto-Mag in his right hand. Bolan holstered it.

"A friend. Will you help me get him out of the camp?"

"I..."

She hesitated. Talk was one thing. Action was another. Bolan saw indecision cross her face.

"Yes or no?"

His hard voice stung her, forcing her to decide.

Laconia pushed himself up on one elbow. He peered up at the tall, husky figure dominating the room.

"Who...who are you?"

"Colonel John Phoenix," Bolan replied, his icy eyes still pinning the girl.

"Code . . . code word?" Laconia held himself up with an effort.

"Stony Man. I'm Stony Man One," Bolan said.

Laconia fell back on the cot. "Th-thank God," he said.

"Well?" The big guy pushed at the girl.

She shook her head. "I . . . I can't help you. I-I'm afraid of what Khatib would do to me if he ever found out. But I won't try to stop you."

"Sh-she's all right," Laconia gasped, the effort costing him a surge of pain.

"She can sound the alarm the minute she's away from us," Bolan snapped.

"I promise. Better—I will swear on the holy Koran that I won't alert the camp," the girl protested.

She was begging Bolan to trust her, to put his life in her hands.

Sure, she was a revolutionary. And she was with one of the most ruthless of them all—Khatib al Sulieman. And Bolan knew that the women in revolutionary movements were usually more fanatical, more dedicated, more intense in their beliefs.

And yet . . . .

He himself had seen her defy the Arab bossman earlier that day. He had seen her bring water to the tortured secret agent. He had seen her wipe down Laconia's agonized face to bring him a small measure of relief from the pain he was suffering.

And now he had found her doing it again, secretly giving aid and comfort to a man who should have been her enemy.

Most important, the words that she had spoken to Laconia—*not knowing she was being overheard by Mack Bolan*—told him that this girl wasn't as hardcase as she thought she was. For the first time in her life, probably, she had come face to face with what it meant to be *personally* involved in the torture of another human being.

Sure, she'd learned how to plant a bomb that would later blow up a building and kill a dozen or more people. But it was one thing to do that—and be miles away when it happened—and another to be right there to watch a man's flesh being slashed by a knifeblade and see the bright, spurting red blood and hear his screams of pain.

Not many people could take that sight without throwing up in revulsion.

For Soraya, apparently, it had been too much.

What was it psychologists called what she was now going through?

Yeah. . . an *identity crisis!*

The girl waited, her large, oval eyes luminous in the glow of the flashlight.

And Bolan suddenly realized that if they were caught, she was putting her life in his hands as much as he would put his into hers if he accepted her offer.

Trust.

Hell, it was a two-way street, wasn't it?

The big guy made up his mind.

"What's your name?"

"Soraya. Soraya Naseer."

"Okay, Soraya. You've got a deal. Is he fit to travel?"

She shrugged. "He has been badly treated. I have no bandages. I have done whatever could be done. His life is now in the hands of Allah. . . and you!"

The big man bent over the cot. In one smooth, powerful movement, he lifted Laconia, slinging him over his shoulder in a fireman's carry.

Soraya went to the door. Hesitated. Turned back.

She said, "How did you get into camp?"

"I cut the links behind the concrete building."

"You wish to go out the same way?"

"Yeah."

"All right, then. I will go out first. If I see anyone in the compound, I'll call out to them. If you hear me, then you'll know there is danger."

Without waiting for the big man to answer, she stepped out into the darkness.

*Well, what do you know*, Bolan thought. In spite of what she'd said a moment before, she *was* going to help—unless she were lying!

Bolan moved to the door. In front of him, there was only the open dark space of the compound. Light rain fell on it, turning the earth black. Soraya was not in sight. She must have gone around the corner of the building.

And then it was time to move out. Time to stick out his neck. Time to find out if he was right in trusting the girl—or whether she'd double-crossed him!

The heavy .44 AutoMag came out of the holster to fill his hand. He flicked off the safety.

There was only one way to find out.

The Executioner took the first step out of the shack into the waiting darkness.

# CHAPTER ELEVEN

WIND BLEW GUSTS of light drizzle into Bolan's face, causing him to squint. His night vision was still acute because he'd used the red-filtered flashlight inside the shack. Bolan slid along the outside wall toward the concrete-block building and his escape route.

Soraya was nowhere in sight.

He tightened his grip on the AutoMag, his keen senses alert for the first rush of footsteps.

Nothing.

He made the back wall, Laconia limp on his shoulder. Bolan knew the poor bastard had passed out. Well, maybe it was better that way. He wouldn't feel the pain of his wounds.

The dead sentry still lay stretched along the base of the wall where Bolan had put him.

The big man drew a deep breath as he prepared for the final move to the chain link fence surrounding the hardsite.

A faint sound reached his ears. He spun, the snout of the .44 AutoMag lifting and his finger tightening on the trigger.

"It's me . . . Soraya."

The girl's shape emerged from the darkness as her whisper slid into his ear.

"I almost killed you." Bolan's low voice barely reached her.

She moved up close to him. "And killed yourself," she said. "If you had pulled the trigger, the sound would have awakened the entire camp."

Soraya gestured toward the body of the dead sentry on the ground.

"You can't leave him here," she breathed. Bolan recognized the fear in her voice. "He will be found and then they will come after you!"

"I wasn't planning on leaving him." Bolan grinned at her even though she couldn't see the expression on his face. "But first I've got to get this one out of the camp."

"I—I must go, now. May Allah watch out for you."

She melted away into the darkness. The sound of the wind gusts and the light drizzle covered her footsteps.

Bolan shifted the weight of the unconscious agent to a more comfortable position. He peered around the corner of the building, just in time to catch sight of the silhouette of another sentry making his turn. The guard's back was toward Bolan. The big guy moved away from the shelter of the building, cutting across the open space to the chain link fence.

Half a dozen quick strides and he was there, sinking to his knees, rolling Laconia's unconscious weight to the ground.

Earlier, Bolan had timed the sentry on his rounds. He had a full minute-and-a-half.

Pushing the cut ends of the chain links apart, Bolan slid through the narrow opening. He turned, his hands gripping the agent's inert body, and pulled him through.

Carrying the limp body in his arms, Bolan moved

up the slope of the hill to the concealment of the boulders.

He was panting when he put down the agent again, but at least they were through.

Through? Bolan grinned at the choice of the word. Not yet.

There was still the telltale body of the dead sentry to be brought out of the hardsite.

TWENTY MINUTES LATER, Mack Bolan dropped the stiffening body of the dead Arab terrorist in a small ravine nearby.

He stood up, breathing hard from the exertion. He'd gone back into the hardsite for a second time to where the corpse lay. After putting the guard's AK-47 on top of the guy, Bolan rearranged the former hardman's arms to hold the weapon in a final embrace. Then he unbuttoned the dead man's shirt and pulled its tail up over the bloody, smashed skull.

In one swift movement, Bolan hefted the corpse into his arms and headed back for the slit in the mesh fence.

Once again, he timed his arrival for the moment when the guard was at the farthest point of his beat. The big guy dropped the body and slithered through the cut. Turning, he grabbed the corpse's heels, pulling it through the fence after him.

Fifty yards from the hardsite, he'd found the ravine and dropped the body into it.

So much for one fanatic whose misguided ideas had led him to a personal Kismet halfway around the world from his homeland. His reward: an unmarked grave and a death still unknown to his fellow conspirators!

Bolan moved back to where he'd left the limp, unconscious figure of Laconia. Again he slung the man over his left shoulder in a fireman's carry. He paused just long enough to check his wrist compass and his watch.

South by southwest was the course to the charcoal burner's shack and the small clearing around it.

The clearing was big enough for a Sikorsky RH-53 Sea Stallion to land on, and close enough to their scheduled rendezvous point for the chopper to divert to it.

In terms of hours and minutes, yeah, there was time to make it long before rendezvous time.

But, the big question was, how long would the damn storm hold off? And how long could Laconia last in the condition he was in?

By this time, Bolan had circled the enemy hardsite. Once on the narrow gravel road that led down the mountainside, he was able to make better time, but every step he took jarred the body of the agent he carried on his shoulder.

Laconia was in bad shape. He needed shelter and medical attention as soon as possible, Bolan knew.

Grimly, the man now known as Colonel John Phoenix strode down the rough surface of the road.

Okay. If he, Bolan, had anything to say about it, the battered, tortured man he carried would get everything he needed to stay alive!

How long ago had it been that Hal Brognola, the

big fed who was the liaison between the Oval Office and the Stony Man group, had passed him the orders? Less than forty, right?

*Find Laconia . . . check!*

*Rescue Laconia . . . check!*

*Or terminate him!*

Well, the third imperative no longer applied.

He had rescued the secret agent.

Now all he had to do was get him safely to the clearing and patch him up as best he could so the man didn't die of his wounds. Keep him alive and safe . . . and hope that the hurricane didn't hit before the Navy chopper got to them . . . or the terrorists found their prisoner was missing and came hunting for the two of them.

So the mission was far from being over just because he'd got Laconia out of the enemy camp!

In fact, it had hardly begun! And it wouldn't end until the secret agent was back in Washington being debriefed—and something was done about the Arab hardsite!

Bolan bent his head into the wind. The light drizzle had got heavier. The wind gusts were more powerful now.

The hurricane had got a lot closer.

The big guy bent his head into the wind and plowed on.

# CHAPTER TWELVE

THE CENTER OF THE STORM moved inexorably closer to the mainland of the South American continent and toward the Panamanian isthmus.

In the eye of the hurricane, there was comparative calm, but around it, in a vast circular movement that covered tens of thousands of square miles, winds howled and blew at speeds of more than 150 miles an hour. The barometric pressure dropped to 27.95 inches of mercury.

Enormous clouds boiled up to 80,000 feet in height—blue-black and purple, churning and roiling. At 40,000 feet, the temperature was 60 degrees below zero. Rain froze solidly almost instantly, turning into sleet, and then fell thousands of feet into warmer air, where the surface melted. Then it was hurled aloft again to freeze once more, each time building up larger and larger pellets of hard ice.

The Caribbean is a shallow sea. On its surface, the howling, screaming winds built up huge waves more than 70 feet high and then sliced across the wave tops, turning them into a blinding white froth and spume that lashed the air into an unbreathable hell.

Nothing could live in the storm.

As it swept across the small islands, it denuded

them of trees and vegetation and buildings. The people who lived on the cays and islands were torn from their shelters, sucked into the air and flung like tiny rag dolls to their deaths.

The sound of the incessant wind was more than a howl, more than a scream. It was the banshee wail of Nature gone completely and totally insane.

On the mainland, in the weather centers, watching the fury of the storm through the camera eyes in satellites high above the earth, meteorologists plotted its direction and speed, thankful that the freak power of the hurricane was headed south instead of north, where it would have wrought its destruction on the land mass of the United States.

But south was where Mack Bolan was.

And the storm would strike the isthmus in only a few hours.

AT STONY MAN FARM, April Rose stared at the large television screen on the wall, which showed the current satellite weather map for Central America.

Beside her, Hal Brognola took in the swirling cloud masses that dominated the screen.

"I don't like it at all," the girl said. The big fed looked quickly at her face. Anxiety was in her eyes.

"How long would you say he had?" Brognola asked.

"Not as much as you gave him," she replied, not taking her eyes from the screen. "The hurricane is moving in faster than anyone expected."

The two of them were in the War Room at Stony

Man Farm. Behind them, Blancanales and
Schwartz were tense, but forcing themselves to
stand quietly.

"We didn't know the storm would move south
so quickly," Brognola said, almost apologetically.

April turned to face him, her eyes flashing. "If
you had, would you still have asked him to go on
this mission?"

The fed nodded his head. "Yeah. We would
have."

"Is Laconia Corporation that important?"

"Not Laconia, no. But what he's learned is important. Damn important."

"Is it worth Mack Bolan's life?"

Brognola saw that the girl was holding back her
tears. She loved the big guy, all right, that was
clear. And it was a shame that she had to suffer
this way, but, hell, in his own way, he loved the
guy, too, and it hadn't been the easiest thing in the
world for him to come out to Stony Man Farm and
ask Bolan to put his neck in jeopardy before the
Stony Man team was ready.

But there were some things you had to do, especially if you had the job Hal Brognola had. There
were times when you put your own life at risk.
Okay, that was expected, and you knew it, and
you accepted the danger as part of the life you'd
chosen to lead.

The hardest part was to order your men into
danger. To ask your friends and comrades—and,
by God, by now Mack Bolan was more than just a
friend to the big fed—to take on an assignment
that both of you knew had only one chance in a
thousand of success.

Before he could answer, the girl put her hand on his arm.

"I'm sorry. I shouldn't have asked you that."

He covered her hand with his own.

"It's okay, April. I understand."

Blancanales spoke up. "Is there anything we can do, Hal?"

The fed turned around. He shook his head. "Not a damn thing."

"When's that Marine chopper supposed to pick him up?"

April answered that one. "It's already on its way," she said, "but..." Her voice trailed off.

"Yeah?"

"The Marines sent it out ahead of schedule because the storm is coming in so fast. We don't even know if the pilot will be able to make radio contact with Striker." Automatically, she used the name she called Bolan when he was in action. "He may not get to the rendezvous point in time."

"If the bossman is anywhere within fifty miles, he'll hear them." Schwartz spoke up in a growl. "That new microminiaturized receiving set is the best available. I worked it up myself."

"That's not the problem," the girl answered quickly. "With this storm, the helicopter may not be able to get within fifty miles of him. Do you know what conditions are like even a couple of hundred miles ahead of Hurricane Frederick?"

Schwartz shook his head.

"Sheer hell," she said. And then she described it.

There was silence for a moment.

"Jack Grimaldi's down there now," Blancanales interjected.

"But nowhere near Striker. He's at Howard Air Force Base, and that's about two hundred miles to the northwest!"

Silence fell. There was nothing for them to say. Worse, there was nothing any of them could do.

Except wait out the night.

# CHAPTER THIRTEEN

AT LEAST IT WAS DRY inside the abandoned hut. Bolan eased the unconscious figure of Laconia onto the ground. Like Bolan himself, the man was sopping wet. He needed to be dried off and warmed.

Ten minutes later, a brisk fire was going in the makeshift fireplace. Heat began to spread through the hut. Bolan stripped the man down, his face showing no expression as ice-blue eyes took in the ugly, brutal wounds inflicted on the tortured flesh.

He bound as many of the wounds as he could, using up the entire contents of his first aid pack, sprinkling sulfa powder on the rest of the wounds, and then worked the limp body into his own dry jungle suit, which had been in his pack since he changed into blacksuit.

He ignored his own discomfort. Laconia's needs took precedence.

Bolan put his hand on Laconia's forehead. The man was burning up with fever! But until he was conscious, the big guy didn't dare try to give him any water.

All he could do was wait until he came around.

THE BIG, LONG-RANGE RH-53 Sea Stallion was flying almost blind, the two pilots continuously fighting the powerful gusts of wind. Rain lashed the Plexiglas of the windshield and drummed on the metal sides of the huge chopper. Gusts slammed it skittering sideways and then lifted it and dropped it a hundred feet at a time.

For two hours, the crew had been clawing their way toward the land mass. They'd taken off from the pitching, tossing deck of the light cruiser hours before the original schedule called for. First, because the light cruiser barely had time enough, even at flank speed, to get out of the path of the hurricane roaring down on them from the north. And second, because unless they made their takeoff then, they wouldn't be able to reach the rendezvous point ahead of the storm.

Now the pilot wasn't so sure they were going to reach the agent called Stony Man One at all. The main rotor tachometer wouldn't remain steady. Periodically, the needle would flick into the high range and then drop back again.

But he had his hands full just trying to keep the chopper straight and level. At his side, the copilot monitored the instrument panel continuously, making constant adjustments, peering down every once in a while to stare at the turbulent waves below them.

"Damnation," he said over the intercom, "I've never seen anything as bad as this!"

"It'll get worse," the pilot flung back. "I can promise you that!"

For the next half hour, they rode the bucking

aircraft in silence, but there was no silence around them. The howl of the big jet turbine engines could not drown out the roar of the wind or the slashing rain.

The copilot pointed down.

"Shoreline," he called out.

"Yeah, I see it. Now where the hell are we?"

"Still on course," said the copilot, pointing out their position on the radar screen mounted on the panel in front of them. "We're okay."

They crossed the shore. Huge waves broke on it, tearing at the land as if to rip it into the sea.

"Gimme a course," the pilot barked.

The chopper angled off, crawling like a monstrous bug across the terrain, never at the same altitude for more than a moment, in spite of the best efforts of the Marine flyers.

Now, as they moved across the isthmus, flying faster than the approaching storm, conditions eased slightly.

Ahead of them, they sighted the dark, brooding mass of the mountain range, the low-lying clouds that obscured its crest, and the rain clouds moving into the higher valleys.

The helicopter lurched as a stronger gust of wind caught it, and the pilot fought the change of course.

The noise of the blades became a momentary scream as the tachometer needle soared and then dropped.

Neither of the men said anything. Both knew there was nothing they could do about it, not until they had the machine on the ground.

"Try him now," said the pilot grimly.

The copilot pulled the microphone to his lips as he switched to the special frequency.

"Birdman to Stony Man One. Birdman to Stony Man One. Do you read me? Over."

Static crackled in his earphones.

"Try him again," said the Marine captain. "Keep on trying him until you raise him."

"Birdman to Stony Man One. Birdman to Stony Man One. Do you read me? Over."

Again and again, pausing for thirty seconds between calls to listen for an answer, the copilot broadcast his appeal.

KNEELING OVER THE MAN, Bolan caught the flicker of twitching eyelids. Laconia stared around the hut for a moment, uncomprehending.

"Relax," said the cool voice. "You're safe now."

The agent tried to lift himself, but he was too weak. Bolan caught him and eased him back.

"You...you're...Co...Colonel John...John Phoenix...right?"

"Right. Okay, I'm going to have to lay it out for you, and it isn't good. You're in rough shape. I don't think we can wait until we get you back to Washington to debrief you."

Laconia smiled weakly at him. "You... mean...I—I might not make it, huh?... S'okay.... Better if I...tell you what...I know.... Important...to get word back. Fast!"

Bolan had to admire the guy. He'd faced up to the fact that he might be dying, that he might not get back alive, and he hadn't blinked an eyelid.

But then, he'd shown how tough he was by taking everything the Arabs could dish out.

"Start talking. What the hell have you found that's so big Washington sent me down after you?"

Laconia drew in a deep breath and gasped in pain. Exhausted, he began talking in a low whisper. Bolan had to strain to hear him.

". . . so then. . . I followed. . . came up. . . here. Stupid of me. . . got careless. . . that's when. . . they caught me." His voice trailed off.

"Okay, okay, but the big question is, what the hell are they going to do with that equipment now that it's set up and operating? What's the word on that?"

Laconia mumbled something too low for Bolan to hear.

Bolan crouched, bending closer, his ear almost touching the guy's lips.

"Say it again. I couldn't hear you."

". . . to control satellites. . . . Planning. . . to take over one of our satellites. . . bring it down. . . ."

Again Laconia's weak voice died away. Bolan looked down at the unconscious man. Poor son of a bitch. He'd really gone through hell. He deserved to rest, but the big guy couldn't let him have it. Not right now.

Bolan wiped the guy's face with his wet handkerchief. He slapped him gently on the cheeks. Laconia's tortured eyes opened.

Bolan demanded, "Why? Why would they hijack a satellite? How could they do it? C'mon, fellow, say it!"

Laconia made the effort. "They...tip it out of orbit.... They know...the self-destruct code...."

*My God, thought Bolan, could these crazy terrorists have figured out a way to intercept one of the most sophisticated secret-information systems in the world? How much do these people KNOW?* The power of the Arab outlaws impressed him, no doubt about it, and the instinct to attack and destroy was starting to course through his blood again.

"Why? You must tell me why they will do this. You must tell me now." Bolan's eyes burned into the glazed stare of a very sick Laconia.

"The satellite monitors oil deployment...you see? They'll know when the tanker...hits Panama...." Laconia groaned, struggling to keep his eyes open and alert. "Then...then they're going...to hit the tanker...."

"What tanker?" His question drilled into Laconia's fading consciousness.

"The next big one...real big one...blow it out of the Canal...." Laconia's mouth was so dry, the words crackled and were lost. His eyes closed.

"They got frog teams...." he whispered. "Maybe...nuclear...."

"Where from? *Tell me.*" Mack Bolan was pleading against the dying of the light in the battered agent. But for now it was all but useless. Laconia's eyelids were closed as if with an enormous weight.

"Want...war...bad...the Hawks...."

Bolan was frozen in thought. There obviously was no time to convey this garbled data to the top brass in Washington. It would only confuse and delay a situation that was sick with merciless, unpredictable savages. With the Canal as number-one target, and a satellite hijacking as the opening shot, there was no time for delay on Freedom's side. Only action would cut through the confusion and pin these bastards to the wall. Action of the right kind. Bolan's kind.

# CHAPTER FOURTEEN

TIME AND THE WEATHER were against Bolan, but there was nothing he could do about either of them.

He had to go back into that hardsite. And he had to do it before the storm hit. Sure, if he waited until the full fury of the storm, he might possibly make his way into the hardsite unseen during the confusion.

But Bolan had seen hurricanes before. Nothing in their path survived—except by luck. What you did was find yourself a big, deep cellar and crawl into it and pray the storm wouldn't suck you out and hurl you a couple of miles down the road!

So whoever it was he would get his hands on had to be found and removed long before the storm hit—because there was also the problem of making the rendezvous with the Marine chopper. So he had no time to waste, not even the few hours he thought he had when he brought Laconia out of the hardsite.

Goddamn! Had they found out that Laconia was missing?

If they had, then the whole camp would be stirred up like a hornet's nest!

Bolan shrugged his shoulders. If that's the way it was, well, so be it!

He'd gone into other sites swarming with armed Mafia hit men and come out in one piece. More than once.

He checked his armament.

Not that he wanted to turn this probe into a hard strike. Far from it. But just in case, he liked to be prepared.

The Stoner M63A1 rifle he carried was fitted in a light machine gun configuration. A 150-round aluminum drum was clipped to its feed mechanism on the right. The weight of the extra 5.56 ammo made it heavy, but it could spew out its tumblers in a steady stream, and every one was deadly.

He had the awesome .44 AutoMag holstered at his right hip. A solid, jacketed slug from the AutoMag could punch its way completely through a cast-iron engine block.

The Beretta's big advantage was that it was silenced. Death spouting from, the muzzle of the Italian beauty was a whisper that its victims never heard.

In the pouch slung from the web belt around his waist were almost a dozen grenades, both frag and flash.

But even with extra clips of ammo for both handguns, Bolan knew it wasn't enough to take on the more than fifty hardmen guarding the terrorist hardsite.

On the other hand, there was such a thing as luck . . . and audacity.

TWENTY MINUTES LATER, just as he was about to intersect the gravel road that led up to the plateau and the enemy camp, his keen eyes registered a familiar sound in the distance.

He halted. Listened. A grin broke out on his face.

Yeah, he was in luck. The sound came from downslope. Grinding its way up the steep, sharp curves of the mountain roadbed was the heavy, constant growl of a V-8 truck engine in low gear, with its four-wheel drive engaged.

Bolan cut through the brush. In less than two minutes, the big man was crouched beside a curve in the road, concealed behind the trunk of a stunted tree.

Rain came down. Overhead, the short branches whipped in the gusts of cold wind.

Even if he were not perfectly concealed, he knew the driver would never see him. Not through this rain.

Bolan held his breath as the truck rounded the curve. A surplus military 6x6, the truck still carried its OD paint. The open body was covered over by a canvas tarp stretched on top of curved ribs. Dim headlights beamed ahead into the falling rain. Not that they did much good.

Windshield wipers beat back and forth across the glass. Bolan caught a momentary glimpse of the driver's intense face as the man hunched over the wheel, fighting the truck's tendency to skid on the slick, wet roadbed.

And then the truck cab was past him and the driver could no longer see him.

Bolan rose, took two running steps behind the rear of the truck, and leaped, his hands clawing for the tailgate.

The Stoner was slung over his back by its sling. He heaved himself up, his stomach slamming into the steel rim, and rolled over into the dark interior.

The rear of the truck skidded, wheels spinning

for a second. Under the tail of the truck, Bolan caught a glimpse of the sheer drop down the mountainside. And then the driver fought the wheels back onto the roadway, and the truck continued to growl its way upward.

Rain thrummed steadily on the canvas tarp overhead.

Boxes filled up almost all the truck's interior. Staggering as the 6x6 flung him from side to side, Bolan pushed a couple of the boxes out of the way and made a nest for himself. Then he pulled a short piece of tarp over him.

Now all he could do was wait—and pray that the guards at the gate were as incompetent as the ones he'd watched earlier.

If they checked the interior of the truck, the way they should, then he was a dead man.

But he was counting on the fact that they were killers, not soldiers. And there was, he knew, one hell of a difference between the two!

After a moment Bolan felt the strain on the truck's engine ease up. The ride became steadier. They were on the plateau approaching the hard-site.

The truck began to slow down. A voice shouted. The truck ground to a stop.

The voices came close. Yeah, they were right outside the truck. Someone was shouting at the driver, and the driver was yelling back.

Bolan didn't have to understand Arabic to know what they were arguing about. There wasn't a military compound in the world where the same thing didn't happen every time the weather was bad.

The guy in the truck didn't want to get out of a dry cab and get soaked just to show his papers.

Someone jumped on the running board. More angry voices.

Bolan pulled the Stoner around and cocked it. His finger slid into the trigger guard, the pistol handgrip filling his palm.

Then the truck engine revved up.

Bolan heard the creak of hinges as the gates were pulled apart. The truck lurched forward, then began moving in low gear through the camp.

He let out a silent sigh of relief. But he knew it was still too soon for him to relax.

Okay, he was back in the camp. But like the lion tamer who shoved his head in the animal's mouth, the trick wasn't in getting it in there—it was getting it out again. All in one piece.

So, for Mack Bolan, the trick would be in getting out of the hardsite.

Alive.

And with whichever one of the top Arabs he could get his hands on.

# CHAPTER FIFTEEN

BOLAN FELT THE TRUCK come to a stop. The engine was shut off. The cab door swung open. A guard's voice challenged the driver. They began to argue.

Gathering himself, Bolan moved out of his hiding place, no longer needing concealment. The canvas tarp darkened the back of the 6x6. He crouched beside the tailgate, ready to make his move.

He recognized the building the truck had parked beside. It was the concrete-block structure that housed the computers, dammit! He wanted to be closer to the shack where he had seen Khatib al Sulieman.

The nightfighter took a moment to orient himself. Now speed and quiet were the important elements.

Catlike, he dropped over the tailgate. His right fist clutched the butt of the Beretta Brigadier he called "Belle." He'd charged the slide before he made his move. The automatic was ready to fire at his slightest touch.

The driver's back was to Bolan, but the eyes of the startled Arab guard fell on him. The hardguy shouted out a command in Arabic. His swarthy hands pulled the assault rifle back to his waist, the muzzle seeking, like a compass needle, to swing toward the big man's torso.

But Bolan's index finger responded reflexively, to stroke the trigger of the Italian-made 9mm beauty. He heard a soft, feline hiss as the silenced slug spun out of the lands of the barrel. It drilled a hole just over the Arab's left eyebrow and exited in an explosion of gristle, gray matter and gore from the back of his head.

By the time the startled driver realized anything was amiss, the Beretta had whispered seductively again, caressed by a second stroke of Bolan's index finger, and once more a cupro-metal projectile lashed out with its deadly sting to slam the guy off his feet. He was dead even as he fell, inert, across the body of the guard.

Bolan leaped forward. In one swift movement, he gathered up two AK-47s, cocked one of them, and spun around in a combat crouch, ready for answering fire—if anyone had spotted him.

No one had. Except for the few on sentry duty, the rain had kept all the hardmen inside, and none of the guards was nearby.

Cold ice-blue eyes measured the situation, scanning the compound through the light rain. Here and there, the yellow glow from electric bulbs spilled out in streaks onto the wet ground.

He spotted the shack he was looking for. Yeah, he was right; it was on the far side of the enemy grounds.

To walk to it across the open area of the compound would have been either foolish or insane, and Bolan—for all his boldness and audacity—was neither a fool nor crazy.

But the answer as to how to get there stood beside him. He went to the back of the truck and took out the Stoner. Along with the two heavy AK-47s, it went into the truck cab.

The two bodies had to be disposed of. One at a time, Bolan heaved the limp, lifeless forms into the back of the 6x6 and then pulled the short tarp over them. These two passengers wouldn't complain, no matter how rough the ride turned out to be!

He stepped up on the running board and slid into the cab. The key was still in the ignition. Bolan goosed the engine into life. Shutting the cab door, he dropped the stick shift into gear and touched the accelerator. The military vehicle ground forward, moving at a steady pace on a direct course across the open compound headed for the shack on the far side of the hardsite.

Bolan forced himself to drive slowly. The hairs on the back of his neck bristled with anticipation. One eye was on the rearview mirror.

What worried him the most was the prospect of a sentry stepping out in front of the truck to stop him. Yeah, if a challenge came, he was helpless. He wouldn't be able to answer the sentry!

The big guy had known since his first soft probe into the encampment that both he and Hal Brognola had made a mistake—a mistake that could now cost him his life!

The guards spoke to each other only in Arabic! And Bolan could speak only English! That meant, the big guy knew, that there was only one course of action open to him if he was spotted and challenged—to swing into action, blasting away with everything he had, and try to fight his way out of the camp!

Every inch of that hundred-yard drive across the ground of the enemy encampment lasted an eternity. At any moment Bolan expected someone to step out from behind one of the galvanized sheet-iron huts and throw a command at him to halt and be recognized.

But no one did.

He pulled the military vehicle around behind the shack nearest the one that was his target and killed the engine. He slid out the cab door to the ground—and froze.

Lights came on at the gate.

Now that the grinding roar of the 6x6's engine was killed, Bolan picked up the sound of another vehicle whining in low gear. The gate was some 50 yards away. The vehicle that pulled in out of the rain and darkness was illuminated by overhead floodlights.

Bolan recognized it immediately. It was a dark blue Land Rover. Mud clung to its lower surfaces. The windshield was obscured except for two pie-shaped patches where the wipers had been flogging away at it. The plastic side curtains were tied down against the drizzling rain.

He saw the sentry come up to the vehicle and then jump to attention and salute. The vehicle dropped into low-low and crawled across the compound, heading directly toward him.

Bolan slid under the shelter of the 6x6 chassis.

But the Land Rover halted in front of the shack.

The driver jumped out—a short, dark man with a heavy black mustache. He ran around to open the passenger door, just as the door to the shack opened. Light poured out of the doorway.

A man stepped out of the Land Rover. In two steps, he was at the door of the shack and then inside.

He was out of sight in a second, yet that second had been long enough for Mack Bolan to get a clear look at him.

Every other man in that hardsite was a Middle Easterner. But not this one. Even though the man's hair was wet, Bolan could see that it was a light, corn-yellow blond.

And he wore a plastic raincoat over a business suit.

Now, who the hell would wear a business suit instead of bush clothes coming up through the steaming jungle from Puerto Obaldía to here?

And who could be so important that the guards at the gate would salute him?

Bolan had another puzzler on his hands.

BOLAN HAD PLANTED three of Schwartz's micro-miniaturized limpet bugs during his earlier probe. Each one of them had a range of up to half a mile. Now, lying hidden under the 6x6, only a few yards away from the hut, Bolan took the receiver out of a pocket of his blacksuit, pulled up the short antenna, and tucked the plug into his left ear.

He switched it on. Nothing. Flicked to the second channel. Still nothing. Again a click of the tiny dial.

Voices blasted in on his eardrum. He turned the

volume down, grinning. He hadn't realized how much the brittle glass of the windowpane would amplify the voices picked up by the bug.

Hell, it was like he was in the room with them!

But, dammit, they were still speaking Arabic!

And they were angry about something.

Then a hard, nasal voice cut across the argument, shutting them up.

"That's enough!" said the voice, in English. "You guys know I don't speak your lingo. If you want to tell me anything, speak English! You all know it!"

A heavy growl answered him.

"We were discussing something among ourselves. It had nothing to do with you."

"Yeah, well I have some things you people must hear, so I'd appreciate it if you'd stop talking among yourselves and listen good. Do I make myself clear, Khatib?"

The Arab's rejoinder was insolent in its tone. "Why have you come, Spinney? Do you think we are children? That we need you to hold our hands? Especially *now!*"

"Knock off the insults, Khatib. I'm here because we've got a big investment in you. A lot of money, a lot of information, stuff you couldn't buy with your right arm anywhere else. Five Scud B nukes from the Russkies, for a start! And we want to see some action. *Now!*"

The Arab laughed.

"Your people! You speak as if you were one of the masters! As if you were a *member* of OPEC, not merely a *servant* for them!"

"I'm a hell of a lot more than that and you know

it. We have the satellite codes, we know which tankers they're tracking, we know how the oil business stands and what will happen if a tanker goes down in the Canal! All you people have is more oil than us, and maybe more nerve. . . .

"So we want the payoff, Khatib. You're going to deliver your end of the bargain, and you're going to do it our way."

"We are ready to strike," hissed the Arab. "But you are too stupid to see that. Have you not observed my progress here?"

He must be smiling, thought Bolan, and with arrogance, maybe menace, but certainly without humor. It was clear from his tone of voice that Khatib intended to do things his way.

"What the hell's the matter with you?" exploded Spinney.

Bolan slithered out from under the truck. Half a dozen crouching strides took him to the window. He rose up to peer in on the scene within the hut.

The man they called Spinney, the blond Westerner, was backed up against the far wall. In front of him, a stocky Arab hardguy stood with his knife unsheathed. One hand held a fistful of the Westerner's suit jacket. The other hand held the honed blade of the knife against the man's throat.

"Ahmad, get away from him!" commanded Khatib.

The husky Arab lowered the knife. Its keen edge glinted in the room's light. In a corner of the room, her eyes wide with fright, was the girl, Soraya.

The blond Westerner pulled his jacket straight. Khatib laughed.

"You're not afraid of Ahmad?"

"I'm not afraid of any of you dumb bastards."

"Be more respectful, please," Khatib said, scowling. "There's no need for you to call us names."

"You deserve it. For Christ's sake—"

"No!" Khatib cut him off. "For Allah's sake! Remember that, my friend. What we do is in the name of Allah and his prophet, Mohammed!"

Spinney laughed cynically. "Come on, Khatib. Be honest! We're all in it for the money. You, for your Hawks of the Revolution. Me, because of the dough I get paid—which is considerable. Now this is how it's gonna be—you're to forget this satellite business for now and get on with the Canal strike."

"How can I hit the Canal without information from the satellite?" demanded Khatib, glaring.

"Get all the information you want, I don't care. What we're after is a superior mess in the Canal, and fast. You hit that supertanker in Lock 3 and there'll be a few million gallons of crude splashing all over the whole country. That's what we want. It'll throw the entire Western world into chaos—"

"I know, I know," muttered Khatib. "But it's the satellite we're after. Can you not imagine, my friend, the humiliation and disgrace of your people when I tip one of their expensive little toys out of the sky?"

"Forget the goddamned humiliation and disgrace!" yelled the enraged Westerner. "Is that all you can think about, you idiot? The tanker's gonna be there in hours, and you guys are staring at the sky with crazy Arabian daydreams. I gotta get back to Puerto Obaldía and get a message out about this...."

Bolan had heard enough. And yet, it wasn't enough.

He'd learned that some acts of violence were about to have worldwide consequences. If the flow of Alaskan and Californian crude was sealed off from the Gulf Coast refineries by the destruction of the Panama Canal, then the OPEC oil advantage would bring Arab domination of the world one step nearer. And if a satellite went, too...

But the exact timing of it he still didn't know.

Spinney did, though. And Spinney would tell him. Yeah, the tough Westerner would talk, all right. It was just a matter of Bolan's getting his hands on the guy and convincing him.

Going back to the port, was he?

Well, there was only one road he could take... and Mack Bolan planned to be on that road.

Waiting.

In ambush.

# CHAPTER SIXTEEN

BOLAN OPENED THE DOOR of the truck, ready to step inside, when he heard the shouted command.

There was no question but that it was directed at him. But that was all he knew. The guard might just have been shouting at him to get his truck out of there, or to ask why the hell he wasn't where he was supposed to be. It made no difference. The thing was, he couldn't answer the guy! This was one time that a bluff wouldn't work.

Okay, so he didn't speak Arabic. But he had something that spoke a universal language!

Bolan reached for the Stoner. Spinning, he dropped from the truck, the weapon in his big hands, his finger on the trigger.

As he landed, he saw there were three of them—not just one! And all three were alert.

They held their assault rifles waist level in firing position, and the big guy knew they were jumpy and would just as soon shoot.

The only thing that held them back was that they didn't know for sure that he wasn't one of them.

In another second, they'd know.

But Bolan never gave them that next second. A contraction of his hand, and a deadly stream of

5.56 tumblers coughed out of the Stoner's muzzle, spitting an invisible line through the night and the rain to hit one of the hardmen gut high, ripping him apart from hip to shoulder, punching him backward in a series of staggering steps.

Even as the man was falling, Bolan twitched the business end of the Stoner in its light machine gun configuration toward the second hardman. The hail of lead tumblers never slowed. Bolan let the muzzle keep rising. Slugs stitched across the terrorist's collarbone, jaw, and forehead.

The third Arab got off part of a burst, but he was at the wrong angle. He let the barrel of the AK-47 rise too high as he yanked back on the trigger. The slugs came nowhere near the jungle master.

The man in black tapped the trigger briefly. It was a half-second burst, but it was enough to send this son of the desert in search of that personal Paradise Muslims believe the Prophet has promised to those of his followers who die in battle.

Yeah, but what they forgot was that it had to be in battle against the enemy for a pure cause, for the purity of Islamic belief, not for their own selfish greed!

Bolan had condemned them to hell and not to heaven!

He'd fired two quick bursts, each less than a second, but he knew it was long enough to alert the camp. The Stoner's hard chatter had ripped apart the quiet of the night, flinging down a challenge to the fifty or so Arab terrorists scattered around the hardsite, announcing that there was an enemy in their midst who played a rougher and harder game than they did. Someone who wasn't afraid of their terror tactics! Someone who'd just as soon stand up to them in spite of overwhelming odds and cut them down in groups or one at a time.

From the periphery of his vision, Bolan glimpsed four figures tumbling out the door of a hut to his right. Crouching now, he twisted his torso around as his trigger finger pressured the release of the sear mechanism of the Stoner M63A1.

A hellfire of tiny 5.56 bullets blistered across the open, rain-filled space between them at a rate of 700 rounds a minute and at a speed of 3,250 feet per second. And the terrorists, stumbling one by one out the doorway, kept on stumbling once they were clear of it. But now they were jerking in a spastic dance of death, their limbs flailing grotesquely, their bodies splotched with sudden gouts of crimson as the slugs tore apart tissue, flesh, and bone.

All over the hardsite, men were racing out other doors, screaming at one another in high-pitched Arabic curses. Some of them nearest the action flung themselves to the ground to return Bolan's fire.

Others, too untrained to know better, raced furiously toward the sound of gunfire, their weapons in their hands.

Bolan swore. There were too many of them for him to make a pitched battle of it. Time had run out on him. He had to get the hell out of the hardsite.

Knees bent, holding the Stoner with its heavy

150-round ammo box in both hands, Bolan spun in a semicircle, his index finger holding down the slim metal of the trigger against the rear of the trigger housing. The weapon bucked and spasmed in his hands, only his powerful wrists and forearms keeping the muzzle down. The big guy found target after target.

Their screams of agony mixed with the chatter of the Stoner and the deeper, harsher bark of the AK-47s now unleashed in his direction.

It was time to retreat. But a smart, strategic retreat often cost the enemy more than in a fixed battle, and Mack Bolan was determined he'd go in his own way.

The nightfighter flung open the door of the truck cab and leaped inside. A twist of the wrist, and the engine roared. He slammed the gear shift lever into first, mashing down on the accelerator as he let up the clutch.

Gunfire started up again. A slug smashed in to shatter the right half of the windshield.

The truck took off in a jerk that snapped his head back. Bolan raced it through the gears, his strong hands twisting the big wheel hard to the left, roaring around behind the shack that was the Arab bossman's field headquarters.

He grinned as the firing behind him cut off. They didn't dare shoot so long as the hut shielded him!

And then the wild run in the rain began. Steering with one hand and peering out into the rainy night, which was lit up only by the glare from his headlights, Bolan unsnapped the cover of the pouch that hung from his web belt, and pulled out a grenade. His left hand still gripped the steering wheel, but he hooked the grenade ring over his middle finger and pulled it loose.

The truck was almost at the far end of the compound. Ahead, the huge mesh bowl of the Intelsat antenna loomed up.

As the truck screamed up to it, Bolan pitched the grenade into the bowl—and then he was past it, waiting for the explosion...and counting... three!...

The grenade blew, but the explosion was on the ground at the foot of the concrete base.

Bolan swore. The grenade had landed in the bowl, all right, but it had rolled right down and out!

And he was too far past it to turn and make a second attempt!

A second grenade was in his hand now, its safety ring pulled. The truck was coming up on the long, barracks-type building, its wheels tearing up mud and dirt as he skidded it closer.

He tromped on the brakes, slowing it, and then he was opposite a window, pitching the grenade into it and racing the deathwagon to get the hell away.

Again the mental countdown...three!...

Behind him an explosion blew the night wide open. Shards of tin razored through the air. The barracks came apart, chunks of it blowing skyward along with fragments of human flesh and ripped limbs and gory pieces of what once were parts of men.

Bolan's ears told him that the explosion was too big to have been just the grenade. The only explanation for the power of the blast was that the grenade had set off a store of explosives. Dynamite, TNT, plastique—it made no difference. It had gone off.

On the big man's face there was a grin at the irony of it.

Terrorists, were they? Yeah, well now they were getting a taste of their own medicine! And he'd just given them a full-course meal of the terror they'd handed out to others!

*Automatic weapons were tearing the hell out of the place....*

At the sound of the firing, the Arab bossman had run out of the headquarters shack with Ahmad and Fuad behind him.

Less than 50 yards away from him, bent in a combat crouch, the machine gun in his hands chattering a litany of shrieking death, was the black silhouette of an avenging demon.

Ahmad slammed his boss to the ground even as Khatib screamed out in rage. A quick burst tore over their heads.

Fuad ran back inside the shack to get his Kalashnikov rifle.

Furiously, Khatib thrust Ahmad away from him. He stumbled to his feet.

The demon in black was leaping into the truck. Khatib screamed at it, shaking a fist impotently.

The truck lurched ahead and then sped off into the darkness. The Arab boss stumbled into one of his hardmen. The man was on one knee, crouched near the shelter of the corner of one of the huts.

Khatib grabbed him by his fatigues, hauling him

to his feet. He slapped the man across his face, snarling a string of Arabic oaths.

"Son of a camel's whore!" he frothed, spittle whitening the corners of his mouth. "Coward! Give me your weapon!"

He snatched the AK-47 from the guy's hands and began to run toward the far end of the compound.

Fuad burst out of the shack. He spotted Khatib and set off after his leader.

As Soraya came out of the hut, a hand caught her by the arm. It was the blond Westerner.

"Wait," Spinney said. "There's nothing you can do."

Soraya pulled away from him angrily.

"Hide, if you are afraid," she snapped at him scornfully.

Spinney grinned at her. "I'm not afraid, baby." He eyed her lush figure. "It's just not my fight, that's all. I've got to get back to the coast tonight. Want to come with me?"

The Arab girl glared at him in disgust. She spun away from him—only to collide with a breathless Ahmad. Ahmad's powerful arm caught her and pulled her in close to him.

Even in the darkness, she could see the wild glare in his enraged eyes. His knife was at her throat.

"Where's the prisoner?" he screamed at her. "What have you done with him?" He shook her violently. "Talk, you bitch!"

She slapped her hand across his face.

"Watch what you call me!"

"What have you done with him?"

"Nothing!" she screamed. "He was in my hut when I came for the meeting with Spinney," she lied in desperation. "I swear it!"

Ahmad released his grip on her. "He's gone! If you know anything about this . . ."

A grenade blew. Ahmad spun around. The blast was at the base of his beloved antenna. He shoved the girl from him and began to run toward the far end of the hardsite.

The truck roared out of the darkness, zigzagging across the muddy open ground, heading for the long barracks building. Soraya saw it run down alongside the barracks, skidding in a tight curve.

And then a powerful explosion ripped apart the air. The building rose and came apart like a slow-motion shot of a flower blooming. Sheets of galvanized tin sailed skyward in a red and yellow burst of angry flame, and in the light of the blast, she saw other things flying through the night. She couldn't identify them for a moment, and then she realized with horror that they were the torn bodies, headless torsos, and arms and legs of men.

For the first time, she felt the paralyzing impact of pure fright—and became aware of how frail her own flesh and blood were.

An involuntary cry of fright burst from her throat.

Spinney grabbed at her arm. Blindly, she struck him away and began to run hysterically toward the truck as it raced in her direction.

All she knew was that she had to get away from Khatib al Sulieman . . . and Fuad . . . and Ahmad . . . and the rest of them. If they ever discovered what she had done, they would kill her with no more compunction than they would the worst of their enemies.

Because, at this moment, she *was* an enemy. What she had done for the tortured Laconia out of mercy—helping him escape—had led to this!

She ran as hard as she could, in total desperation.

She wanted to live.

MACK BOLAN SAW the running figure as it came toward him, and he turned the nose of the truck, aiming for it.

One more terrorist, he thought grimly.

One *less* terrorist!

The roar of the truck engine filled his ears. Shots ripped at the truck in chattering bursts from AK-47s around the compound. The blast of the explosion still reverberated in the air. The hardsite was a hellground of battle. As in any firefight, men untrained to combat had a tendency to hold down the trigger of their weapons and fire off an entire clip at one time—without aiming.

Short, aimed bursts. That lesson had to be drilled into every recruit again and again. *Aim and squeeze and let go. Aim and squeeze and let go.*

But most of the time you couldn't teach them that lesson. The sound of their guns firing reassured them that they were doing something.

Bolan grinned mirthlessly at their fire inefficiency, and jammed the accelerator down harder.

He was within ten yards of the running figure when he realized it was the girl.

Bolan swore, twisting the wheel of the truck as he slammed on the brakes.

The girl just stood there as the big vehicle skidded in the mud.

At the last minute, she tried to leap aside, but fell to the ground. The truck lurched to a stop beside her.

She was on her knees, screaming out to him.

*"Take...me...with...you!"*

The words caromed into Bolan's ears. He locked the brake, leaped to the ground beside her, knowing that what he was doing was insane, knowing that he should have gone on racing for the gate, and the hell with her. She was one of them, wasn't she?

But her pitiful cry for help had reached him. Brown eyes, blank with shock, stared helplessly up at him.

The big guy swore and bent down, and his hands heaved her up and into the cab of the truck in one swift, fluid motion. And then he was behind the wheel himself, throwing off the brake, gunning the 6x6, and racing for the gate, the heavy mud tires of the truck flinging clods of rain-soaked earth behind it.

Ahead of him, through the metronomelike action of the one windshield wiper still fighting the rain, Bolan made out a lone guard at the gate. The guy was kneeling, aiming his AK-47 at the oncoming truck.

Rain whipped in the broken half of the windshield, the spray cold on Bolan's face. In one hand he held the bucking steering sheel. With the other he hauled the big .44 AutoMag out of its holster.

A finger slid into the trigger guard, and the gun bucked hard in his fist, sending a slug through the open, broken glass, directly at the hardguy's chest. The bone-crusher slug blasted the guy's rib cage apart even as he made ready to fire, flinging him back against the gate posts like a rag doll.

The gate loomed up in front of them. Bolan had time only to fling his arms around the girl and pull her into him as protection for her face in case the windshield shattered even more.

In four-wheel drive, the engine screaming at top revs, the blunt nose of the 6x6 crashed through the wire and wood of the gates, crumpling them like a penny matchbox hit by a fist.

They went through!

Behind them, angry guns continued to blast away in futile attempts to reach them.

Bolan raced the truck down the incline, careening into the first curve of the roadbed that twisted its way down the mountainside. A moment later he was out of sight of the Arab camp.

His foot down hard on the accelerator, the big guy skidded the heavy 6x6 around the curves in slewing, sliding turns.

Behind him, the broken, torn bodies that littered the hardsite left proof that the Executioner was still a master at his trade.

# CHAPTER SEVENTEEN

BOLAN SLOWED DOWN and switched on his headlights. The roadbed clung to the mountainside, twisting and turning in a series of switchbacks. Nowhere at all was it wide enough to take at any significant speed.

Half a mile down the road, he stopped the truck.

He had time. At least ten minutes. He didn't think they'd get organized for a pursuit in less than that.

The big guy turned to the girl crouching on the seat beside him.

"All right," he prodded, "how come your sudden change of mind? You could have come with me earlier without risking your neck the way you did."

He saw her shiver, and not from the chill.

"They...Ahmad found out that...that your spy...."

"Laconia?"

"Is that what you call him? We didn't know. Ahmad found he was missing....Ahmad is insane. He would have killed me if he learned I had...helped you."

Bolan was silent. He was going to have to trust this girl. Yeah, he'd trusted her once before and she'd come through, but he was going into combat

now. It was a different kind of trust, and he had to
know it was there—totally! So far, all she'd told
him was that she'd fled the Arab hardsite because she feared for her life.

It wasn't enough.

As if she'd read his mind, Soraya went on.
"I...I couldn't stay there any longer. After you'd
left...after I had a chance to think about what
they'd done to...to Laconia, as you call him, I
began to see there was no difference between
them and...and...*animals!*"

She spat out the last word.

"From the time I was little, I was taught that
the Israelis were beasts. That they had stolen
Arab land...killed Arab people. That ours was a
*jihad*—a holy war—against them. But we're no
better. We're worse, aren't we? To...to torture a
man the way Ahmad tortured this Laconia! To set
off bombs in stores...on busy streets! In the
name of Allah, how can we take pride in what we
believe, if this is the way we act!" she burst out.

Bolan said nothing. He let the girl spill out her
inner feelings. They came in a torrent of words, as
if by telling him everything she could cleanse
herself of the filth she'd been a part of.

"I...I couldn't take any more. I couldn't
believe anything that Khatib said. Lies! All lies!
Spinney said it was for money and Khatib agreed
with him. But I know it's more than that! Khatib
wants power! That's all! And he doesn't care how
he gets it! He'll murder...and destroy...and
kill! Just so long as he can become important in
the Arab world! Even our holy cause! He has be-
trayed that, too—all for his own personal gain!"

She drew in a long, shuddering breath. "I hate him! I hate everything he stands for!"

"And everything you stood for?" Bolan asked quietly.

The girl lifted her head proudly and looked him right in the eyes. Her voice echoed in the silence of the truck's dark cab.

"No! I still believe in my people. I believe they should have what they lost. I believe in a homeland for Palestinians. But this is not the way to get it! Not by murder...or assassination...or bombings and killing of innocent people! We have to sit down and talk it out. Reasonable people talking to reasonable people! That's the only way peace will ever come to my homeland!"

"Will you help me stop them?" Bolan asked.

"Khatib?"

"Him and the others."

It was the ultimate test.

Soraya bit her lip. She took a long time to answer. Then she nodded slowly.

"Y-yes. I must."

"Then tell me what Khatib's plan is. He has an Intelsat antenna focused on a space satellite, hasn't he?"

"Yes."

"Why?"

"Because it gives him information on the whereabouts of every gallon of U.S. crude oil being piped or transported anywhere in the world."

"Well, that makes him too powerful an animal for me. How the hell did he crack our satellite codes?"

"Spinney's people—they are the ones that buy

the information from your government, and they're the ones who paid to put the satellites there five years ago.''

"You know everything about this setup?'' Bolan stared hard at Soraya.

"No. Only that Khatib is obsessed with destroying a satellite. It is his dream. Now Spinney wants him to destroy the Panama Canal instead... blow it up with the Scud B missiles we—I mean Khatib's men—have been given by Spinney. They are all crazy. At first I thought it was to be a great action for my people, but now—now it is crazy, it is all out of control.''

"My view entirely, young lady,'' mused Bolan, as if to himself. He was becoming increasingly disturbed by the wild dimensions of Khatib's scheme. No ordinary military offensive would be swift enough and invisible enough to eradicate this madness. It would have to be him—on his own—now.

Rain pelted the steel top of the truck cab and drummed on the taut canvas over the body.

Over the steady noise, a new sound came faintly to Bolan's sharp ears. From behind he heard the grind of engines descending the hill in low gear.

Spinney had said he needed to get back to Puerto Obaldía as soon as he could. But Spinney wasn't alone, not from the sound of it. It seemed as though he had an armed escort.

Bolan kicked over the engine and threw the truck in gear. He knew he could race them to the base of the mountain and make his getaway. He was a better driver than any of his pursuers.

Or, he could leave the truck and head back for Laconia with the girl.

But he hadn't come so far just to run from them.

He still wanted to learn what Spinney knew.

Bolan dropped the gear lever into reverse. He backed the truck so that its tailgate was jammed against the slope of the mountainside.

Now the heavy 6x6 was slanted across the road-bed from one side to the other, blocking it completely. It couldn't be seen until the first of Spinney's escort vehicles rounded the sharp curve only a few dozen yards back.

If they were going at any speed at all—well, hell, that was their lookout, wasn't it?

His hand reached for the Stoner leaning against the seat between him and the girl.

"Let's go," he said.

She caught his forearm.

"Wait."

The big guy eyed her suspiciously. Had she changed her mind?

"I said I would help you. Well, I'll keep my promise. But—I cannot..."

"You can't *what*?"

"I cannot shoot my...my brothers." She gulped out the words as if afraid of the big guy's reaction.

Bolan's answer was a cool grin.

"I'll do my own shooting, baby," he retorted. "You just come along and keep your head down. Okay?"

She hesitated and then nodded.

Bolan climbed out of the truck into the light rain, the Stoner in his hand.

In the truck behind him were the two Arab guards he'd killed earlier—and their AK-47s.

The AKs might come in handy.

He pulled them out and slung them over his shoulder. Soraya was standing in the rain, shivering.

"Follow me," he snapped at her, and plunged ahead up the slope of the mountain. Behind him, he heard the girl scrambling and clawing her way up the rocky ground.

Twice he paused to reach back and grab her arm to help her over a tangle of boulders. Each time, he was conscious of the soft female figure under the rough cloth of the fatigues she wore.

A flat outcrop of rock projected from the slope about ten feet higher than the roadbed. Bolan settled himself into it, pushing Soraya down behind him.

"You'll be safe here," he assured her. "Just keep your head down."

Bolan barely had time to settle himself, the two AK-47s lined up beside him, the butt of the Stoner pulled tightly into the pad of flesh at his right shoulder, when the first vehicle of the convoy nosed around the corner.

## CHAPTER EIGHTEEN

HEADLIGHTS STABBING out into the darkness, the lead truck came around the curve, going too fast for the treacherous road.

Behind it came the mud-spattered Land Rover.

Spinney!

And behind the Land Rover crawled the third vehicle in the escort convoy—another 6x6, whose lights illuminated the squat, high body of the Land Rover.

Yeah, Spinney was in it! Bolan could see him outlined clearly against the light shining in the rear window.

It was time to close the trap.

There was a brief moment when the driver of the lead truck sighted the 6x6 parked full across the roadbed. Bolan saw the startled look on his face.

He must have slammed down desperately on the brake pedal, but the truck didn't slow down at all.

The big guy caressed the trigger of the Stoner, and the brake pads never had a chance to touch.

Like a swarm of enraged bees, the 5.56mm tumblers smashed the windshield of the lead truck into a thousand shards of shattered, razor-edged glass; they then tore apart the driver's skull in an explosion of bone and gristle and gore.

The short burst was enough to turn that short stretch of road into a scene of hellish destruction. Even while the sound of the gunfire was still in the air, the lead truck plowed full bore into the 6x6. The tortured screech of rending metal ripped the air, as the mass and momentum of the heavy vehicle carried them both over the lip of the mountain roadway.

First one, then the other, tipped over the edge to disappear from sight. And now the night was laced with the trailing, fading screams of those terrorists trapped in the back of their truck as they fell helplessly to their doom.

For Bolan, there was no time to waste in contemplating their deaths.

He put a short burst of fire into the front tires of the Land Rover to immobilize it. A second quick burst smashed the hell out of its engine compartment.

And now it was time for the second truck. Once more the Stoner chattered and slammed against Mack Bolan's shoulder. Glass shattered. Truck brakes screamed hotly. The big vehicle skidded, slithering wildly from one side to the other. It slammed into the back of the Land Rover as it came to a halt.

Men leaped wildly from the back of the truck, dropping over the tailgate, assault weapons clutched in their hands.

Only the driver, slumped over his wheel, didn't move. Not with a burst through his chest!

Bolan aimed at the first group of terrorists. Two shots cracked out of the Stoner—and that was it.

The bolt slammed back, locking open as a sign its ammo drum was empty.

Bolan dropped the weapon to seize the nearest AK-47. It was quicker than trying to reload the Stoner with one of the clips in his web belt.

The hoarse, deep, coughing grunt of the Kalashnikov punctured the falling rain and the screams of the enraged hardmen.

The Kalashnikov was a heavier gun than the Stoner, weighing better than nine pounds without a loaded clip, but it was a gun that Bolan had used many times during his combat tours in 'Nam, and he was as familiar with it as he was with any American or NATO weapon.

The big guy fired off the thirty-round clip of 7.62 slugs in six quick, aimed bursts, taking out the nearest of the charging Arab toughs. He grabbed up the second AK-47 to repeat the lead messages that spoke a universal language—death! Yeah! Something short and terse they'd have no trouble understanding!

Tumbling bodies sprawling to the ground in midstride told the Executioner that his dispatches had been received. Return reply not requested.

But others answered in their place. From various points behind the stalled vehicle, return fire laced the night. Jacketed slugs howled and whined in wild ricochets off the rock of the slope behind the big guy.

Reaching into the pouch, Bolan took out a couple of frag grenades. He pulled pins, letting the spoon handles fly off.

In the few seconds that Bolan ceased fire, the Arab terrorists grew bolder. Two of them leaped from behind the cover of their truck, AK-47s aimed at his position. Slipping and scrambling through the rain in the muddy gravel of the road-bed, they ran toward him, their faces glaring with fanatical hatred, howling a high-pitched Arabic scream as they ran.

"*Allah!...Allah akhbar!...*"

Bolan heaved the first grenade and then the second. Both grenades were in the air at the same time, one arching over the truck to come down behind it, the other dropping just in front of the ledge.

The twin explosions blew apart the rain and blasted the truck. The heavy vehicle lurched to a halt on its blown-out tires. Running men were blown off their feet.

Only two of them rose, groggily, their bloodied faces still enraged as they stumbled forward with their AK-47s pointing up at their attacker.

Bolan's right hand flashed to his side. The big .44 AutoMag leaped into his fist. Now it was one on one, with Bolan against the two crazed fanatics.

Half rising, the solid weight of the AutoMag filling his fist, Bolan swept smoothly into firing position. The gun bucked twice.

Two hundred and forty grains of solid slug hit like an express train, blasting through flesh and bone as though they were nothing, hurling each body backward and to one side, each crashing lifelessly into the mud.

Bolan followed them with the muzzle of the .44. Neither of them moved.

And now, almost startling after the brief

clamor of the short firefight, there was silence—silence so acute that Bolan heard the stifled whimpering of the girl lying behind him.

"It's over," he growled. "Stay where you are."

Quickly, he slid down from the rocky outcrop overhanging the road. The AutoMag was still in his fist.

Carnage was the word that best described the scene. The Land Rover's headlights were still on, lighting up the hellground that Bolan had created.

In the roadway, the two Arab hardmen who'd tried to attack his position lay sprawled in their own blood and ripped flesh.

Bolan bypassed the Land Rover. In the cab of the truck, his head a bloody mass and his chest blown open by the 5.56 Stoner tumblers, the driver lay dead. Beside him, another terrorist youth lay slumped against the gear shift lever.

Bolan walked behind the vehicle.

Except for one of the terrorist hardmen, they were all stilled forever.

The youth looked up at Bolan as the big man stood over him. Dying, the guy's eyes were still hot with anger. Bolan could almost feel the intensity of the youth's hatred. Neither in Vietnam nor in his long fight against the Mafia had Mack Bolan encountered such vitriol.

The big guy looked down for a moment before he put the AutoMag to the terrorist's head. It was almost as if the Executioner was saying a silent prayer for the young terrorist's soul. And then he stroked the trigger and blew away bone and brain and whatever hatred was still in there.

Now, except for the fall of the raindrops, there was no sound on the mountain road.

Bolan walked around to the Land Rover.

The driver was dead. Beside him, slumped against the seat, was the blond Westerner, Spinney.

Bolan reached in and felt his pulse.

Okay. He was still alive. He pulled him from the vehicle and put him in the road, his back leaning against the rear wheel.

Rain fell on Spinney's pale, hard face. Bolan waited. In a minute he saw the man's eyelids flicker, then open. Spinney stared at him uncomprehendingly.

Bolan shoved the muzzle of the AutoMag against Spinney's forehead.

"I want some information," the big man rapped out, his voice hard. "And I don't have time to play around. What's that bastard Khatib planning?"

Spinney shook his head. His eyes began to close. Bolan slapped his face with his left hand.

"Talk, damn you!"

Spinney made a sound in his throat. A bubble burst from his mouth, a gob of red froth spilling down his chin.

Bolan reached out and grabbed him by his hair. He lifted the guy's head roughly.

"I said, talk, damn—" and cut off in midsentence.

*Talk...*

No, Spinney wouldn't talk to him. Or to anyone—ever. Blood gouted from under his chin in a thin stream. It came from a deep wound in his throat, and sticking out of the wound was a jagged piece of metal.

Even as Bolan let go of the blond Westerner's head, the guy fell over on his side—dead.

Bolan collected half a dozen fully loaded 7.62 ammo clips for the AK-47s before he walked back to the outcrop to pick up his weapons and the girl. He left the bodies littering the scene as a message to the Arab boss.

Soraya was on her feet. As Bolan came close, he could see the horror written on her face. Her body was tense, trembling with agitation.

"You ready to go?" he asked, his voice icy. He saw she was on the verge of hysteria—even a hint of softness or sympathy on his part would bring it on.

She nodded, unable to speak.

Bolan slung the Kalashnikovs and the Stoner over his shoulder. He checked his wrist compass. They were about a mile and a half from the charcoal burner's hut where he had left Laconia.

In the gray spatter of the falling rain, soaked to the skin, Bolan set off down the mountain road. The girl followed him.

Behind the death specialist, the bodies in the mud were slowly being washed clean of blood by the rain falling from the gathering storm.

But it would take a hell of a lot more than just rain to wash them clean of their sins.

# CHAPTER NINETEEN

THE RASPING SOUND of Laconia's breathing filled the hut as Bolan flicked on his flashlight and entered. Laconia still lay on the ground, Bolan's rolled-up jungle suit under his head as a pillow.

Soraya pushed past the big guy to rush to Laconia's side. She put a cool hand on his forehead.

"He's burning up with fever," she gasped. "Isn't there anything..."

"I've already given him penicillin and put sulfa on his wounds," the man in black replied. "Just keep his head wet."

Bolan put down the weapons he'd brought back. As he was unclipping the web belt from around his waist, the thin, high-pitched *beep-beep* of the miniature radio set in his black fighting outfit brought the big guy to an immediate alert.

He pulled it out, flicking the switch to "Receive."

Static exploded. Then he made out the words.

"...*Man One...Birdman...to Stony Man One... Do you...read me? Over.*"

Bolan brought the set to his lips.

"This is Stony Man One...Stony Man One to Birdman... I read you.... Over." He repeated the call. "Stony Man One...to Birdman...I read you...one by one....Over."

Another burst of static, and then: "...*location...find....*" Crackling destroyed the rest of the transmission.

Then it came a second time.

"*Turn on...location finder....*"

Without bothering to acknowledge the call, Bolan grabbed up his backpack and pulled out a small black box no larger than a cigarette pack. He pulled up the miniature antenna and activated the set, ducking out into the rain to set it on the ground near the hut.

His radio crackled and spit. This time the voice came in loud and clear.

"*Birdman...to Stony Man One.... We've got you.... Estimate arrival...ten minutes... Do you copy?*"

"Roger..." Bolan replied. "Estimate your arrival...ten minutes."

"*Birdman to Stony Man One... You're coming in better.... Will you be ready to depart...with passenger?*"

Static bleeped out some of the words.

"Say again," Bolan requested.

"*Will you...be ready...for...pickup?... Do...you...have...passenger?*"

"Affirmative on passenger... Come on in and pick him up."

Another voice cut in. "Stony Man One...this is aircraft commander talking.... We have orders to pick up two men—"

The transmission suddenly ended.

Bolan rapped out, "Birdman...come in, Birdman... Do you read me?"

Nothing. Then: "*Stony Man One...Stony Man*

One.... This is Birdman.... Light your flares....
Light your flares...."

The big guy caught the note of repressed panic
in the copilot's voice. Even as he dug into the bot-
tom of his backpack for a couple of stub flares, the
voice went on.

"We have...trouble with...rotor blade...
governor.... Light your...flares...."

Bolan grabbed up the two cylinders and raced
out into the middle of the clearing. The mini-
receiver was in his pocket, but the sound was loud
enough for him to hear the voice clearly.

"Birdman to Base...Birdman to Base....
This is a May Day...May Day.... Do you read
me?"

Silence.

Bolan shoved a flare into the soggy ground and
pulled the self-igniting tab. Hissing and sputter-
ing, the flare burst into a bright red flame.

He ran 20 yards and planted the second flare
and ignited it.

"Affirmative, Base...this is a May Day....
rotor governor...will attempt landing.... Do you
have...a fix?"

Bolan realized that there had been no need for
the copilot of the chopper to switch to the distress
frequency of 121.5 megacycles. Base—whatever
it was, probably a light cruiser—had been
monitoring the chopper's transmissions to him!

"Affirmative on that, Base...will be unable to
take off...this is a May Day...."

The chopper's transmission was much louder.
Bolan thought he could hear the *whapping* sound
of whirlybird blades.

"Birdman. . ." he called into his mike. "I think I hear you to the southeast."

"Roger, Stony Man. . . you're loud and clear. . . . We have the flares in sight. . . . But we have. . . a problem. . . . Stand by. . . ."

The voice went off the air. From his position near the hut, Bolan scanned the darkness to the southeast, trying unsuccessfully to peer into the curtain of rain and night.

Out in the clearing, the flares crackled on, spitting intense incandescent globules of sparks along with a powerful reddish orange glare.

And then faintly at first, but growing louder, came the irregular *whup-whap, whup-whap* of helicopter blades. In a moment Bolan made out the dark bulk of the big Sea Stallion chopper emerging from the rain clouds and the night.

It was no more than 100 feet above the terrain, coming toward him at an angle, the mass of its slab-sided body canted as it fought the crosswind gusts.

Sound pounded the air, but there was something radically wrong with it. It came in a rising and falling pitch, and then as the chopper neared the ground, the sound rose to a howling scream.

The huge machine lurched in the air, dropped a dozen feet, straightened out, and slewed off to one side.

Bolan swore out loud, sickened at the thought of the forthcoming crash.

But the Marine pilot was good. Damned good. Or damned lucky.

The enormous hulk whipped back, canted only slightly, and dropped the remaining few feet to land with a jolting, tearing crash on the far side of the flares.

Bolan was racing across to the doomed bird even as it came down those last few feet.

It lay partly on its side, one of its skids ripped loose by the impact. Its rotor blades were still, but they had an unnatural curl to their tips. Fluid gushed from the chopper's fuel tanks.

Bolan leaped up, caught a crossbar, and stood on top of the hulk. He grabbed the cockpit door, heaving with all the power at his command, wrenching the door open.

A blood-streaked face looked up at him, dazed.

He reached down to catch the pilot under his armpits. Bodily, he lifted him out of the wreck.

"Co—copilot..." the major gasped. "Get... get...copilot..."

Bolan dropped into the cockpit of the helicopter. The copilot lay unconscious across the cyclic stick. Quickly he unsnapped the man's harness. With one foot planted against the seat back, he heaved the man free, shoving him up and out through the open cockpit door.

He dropped down to the ground after the body.

The Marine major stood off to one side, holding his hand to his blood-streaked head.

"Hu-hurry..." he gasped. "Tanks are...ru-ruptured!"

Bolan slung the copilot to his shoulder, staggering away from the wreck, the pilot close at his heels.

Like some prehistoric insect, the machine lay almost on its side. One minute it was there, a black silhouette in the night, and the next minute a soaring ball of orange and red flame leaped up into the darkness.

The thick, solid *whoomp* of the explosion hit Bolan, knocking him to the ground with his burden. Thank God for the terrain and the tree cover and the fog—this disaster should go undetected beyond a few thousand yards, he guessed.

He was unhurt. He rolled over to kneel beside the unconscious copilot. The Marine major staggered to them.

"How...how is he?"

Bolan's hands checked the body.

"He's hurt," he said, standing up. "Hurt bad."

The major took his bloodstained hand from his head. His other arm hung limply from his shoulder.

"Shit," he said in disgust. "What do we do now?"

# CHAPTER TWENTY

AT HOWARD AIR FORCE BASE, on the Pacific edge of the Canal Zone, Jack Grimaldi paced impatiently back and forth in the guest room he'd been given in the BOQ.

For the past hour, he'd been waiting for word to be relayed that the Sea Stallion chopper had picked up Mack Bolan and was on its way back.

Once more, he glanced at his wristwatch. The hands seemed to have become glued to the same position.

There was a knock on the door.

"Come in," he growled.

A young first lieutenant entered. Before he could speak, Grimaldi snapped at him, "Well, is there any word?"

The officer said, "Mr. Grimaldi, the Group Intelligence officer would like to have a word with you. If you'll follow me?"

"Dammit, have you people heard anything?" Grimaldi's face was set in a hard scowl.

"That's what he wants to brief you on," said the lieutenant politely. "If you'll come this way, sir..."

The Group G-2 was a tough, chunky-bodied Major. On the left breast of his shirt were two rows of fruit salad—ribbons and decorations that told his military history. Grimaldi, himself an ex-pilot of Vietnam vintage, scanned them and was impressed.

The major was terse.

"We've got word," he commenced the minute Grimaldi stepped into the room with him. "It's not good."

A full-scale map of the Panamanian isthmus, including the northern part of Colombia, covered the wall behind him.

He stepped to it. His finger touched the chart northeast of the Golfo de Urabá.

"A long-range Sea Stallion chopper took off from the deck of a light cruiser about here, several hours ago. Because of deteriorating weather, the cruiser had to get the hell out of the area. The plan was for the chopper to make landfall about here..." His forefinger moved southwest, coming to a stop near Acandi. "And then go inland to where Stony Man One was dropped off yesterday."

Grimaldi listened intently, waiting for the bad news the G-2 was going to drop on him.

"They were to have picked him up, along with his passenger, and then continue on westward to the Gulf of Panama, which would get them away from the oncoming hurricane. Somewhere here—" again his forefinger stabbed at the map "—there's a carrier on patrol. That was to have been their destination."

"They never made it," said Grimaldi, making a flat statement. "Right?"

The major didn't answer him directly.

"There was constant communication with the

helicopter and its crew via radio relay. I don't know if the communication was bounced off a satellite or whether there was an aircraft circling at altitude midway between your man and the carrier. Doesn't make any difference. A few minutes ago, we received this. It's from the tape of the last messages the carrier picked up from the chopper."

His finger pressed the "Play" button on the tape recorder on his desk. Static filled the room and then voices broke through, and Grimaldi listened to the final exchange between Mack Bolan and the crew of the Sea Stallion whirlybird.

The voices on the tape ceased abruptly. The major punched off the machine, but in Grimaldi's head, the last words continued to echo: *"This is a May Day... May Day.... We have a problem."*

Yeah, they'd had a problem all right, and no one had to tell Grimaldi, a former combat pilot, that they were probably in serious difficulties. Years after his war experience he could feel the same surge of emotion toward them. A deep feeling of respect. Respect because they had put their lives on the line in the performance of their duties.

The major was talking. "Washington's been notified. The brass instructed us to brief you."

He hesitated for a second. "I'm sorry, Mr. Grimaldi. I understand that Stony Man One was close to you...."

"What the hell are you implying?" Grimaldi interrupted. "He's not dead—yet!"

"He might as well be." The major bit off his words. "Now that the chopper is down, we have no way to get him out. And with the approach of the hurricane—"

"Hold it! Who said there's no way for him to get out?"

The G-2 was taken aback. "Well, sir," he began formally, "I doubt if we can risk another crew to make the pickup. So . . ."

Grimaldi wasn't listening to him. In two strides he was at the wall map, his eyes taking in the details. He measured the distance from the Canal airbase to the Serranía del Darién range. His finger found the mountain peak Mack Bolan was on. Okay, no problem there. A hundred seventy-five miles was well within range. Taboga Island, about ten miles southeast of Howard Air Force Base, had a VORTAC station, with a high frequency VHF omni-directional signal capacity. Farther east, across the Gulf of Panama, there was a VOR station on La Palma. These stations were all he needed for air navigation. Hell, he'd practically overfly it on a direct course from Howard AFB to where he wanted to set down.

Satisfied, he spun around.

"Major, are you aware of that cable from Washington about me?"

The major nodded. "I am. We're to provide you with all possible assistance."

Grimaldi grinned. "Yeah. Well, I want a Cobra warmed up and waiting for me on a hardstand within the next half hour. Full tanks. Fully armed."

The G-2 began a protest. Grimaldi cut him short. "Just do it, Major," he snapped. "Don't waste time arguing. It'll be your ass if I report back you refused to cooperate! Got it? And while you're at it, leave word at the armament shack that I'm stopping by. There's some equipment there I'd like to take along."

"It's sheer suicide," the Air Force officer protested. "You'll never beat out that hurricane. And a small chopper in winds like that—hell, man, if you want to kill yourself, put a gun to your head and pull the trigger. Why do it the hard way?"

Grimaldi never heard the last of that protest. He was on his way out of the major's office to pick up the flight equipment he'd left in the BOQ room.

Time was now racing for him. There were navigation charts to pick up at Operations. There would be a quick but thorough briefing on the weather at Meteorology. There was a crystal he had brought down with him that had to be installed in the Cobra's communications systems, one that would match the set Bolan carried. Yeah, and a load of other items from Armament he was sure Mack Bolan would be able to find a use for, once he got to him.

The half hour would barely be time enough to get it all together.

And yet, he burned with impatience because the half hour was still a half hour too long.

IT WAS FOUR-THIRTY in the morning. They had been up all night getting infrequent reports, but mostly just spending their time waiting.

At Stony Man Farm, Schwartz put down the internal telephone that connected him with the communications room. He looked up at Brognola and April.

"That was the Pentagon," he said. "They're madder than hell. Grimaldi's conned the brass down at Howard into supplying him with a Cobra helicopter. Some four-star general just told me that when they'd said 'all possible assistance,' they didn't mean a fully-armed, million-dollar fighting helicopter like a Cobra!"

"Fully armed?" That was Brognola.

"Yeah." Schwartz nodded. "Do you know the Cobra, Hal? It's the helicopter version of a fighter aircraft. It's pure, mean murder. It can do everything, including a vertical dive out of a power climb, and when it comes down with all guns blazing. . ." He shook his head. "You just don't want to be in front of it."

Schwartz grinned. "Grimaldi's got this one loaded with everything but a nuke warhead. Air-to-ground rockets, for instance."

"What the hell. . ."

Schwartz's grin broadened. "Looks like Jack Grimaldi's out to start a one-man war."

"He's insane!" April burst out. "Even if he can get to Striker, there's no way Jack can get back through that hurricane! Not in a helicopter! He'll kill them both!"

Blancanales came over and touched her on the shoulder.

"Hey," he said, "take it easy, April. You gotta have faith. If anyone can do it, Grimaldi's the guy."

She turned to him. "Pol, you know it yourself! There's not one chance in a million that he can make it. . ."

Blancanales put his finger across her lips.

"Don't say 'impossible,' baby," he said. "The Sarge doesn't know that word. And neither does Jack. Not if the bossman's in trouble."

He saw the glistening of tears in her eyes. She turned her head away.

Deep down, he felt as sick as she did, but he wasn't going to express his fears. Not in front of them, ever.

But a prayer wouldn't hurt now, would it?

So, silently, Blancanales offered up a silent petition to the Big Guy. The One up there.

## CHAPTER TWENTY-ONE

KHATIB AL SULIEMAN WAS FURIOUS. Anger smoldered in his dark eyes as he raged back and forth in the confines of the headquarters shack.

"Camel dung!" he screamed in Arabic at his two lieutenants. "That's what you are! Both of you! Eaters of dog turds! Fornicators of diseased sheep!"

Ahmad flushed hotly. He fingered the hilt of his knife. Fuad put a restraining hand on his arm, gripping it tightly.

"We did the best we could," Fuad protested.

Khatib turned on him.

"One man!" he shouted. "Just one man! And look what he did to us!"

Fuad bit his lip.

"How did he get into camp?" the head Arab demanded. "Ahmad, you are in charge of security. How did this man get past the gates?"

"He cut his way in," the swarthy hardguy answered. "We found the place in the fence where he severed the chain links."

"No," Fuad spoke up, puzzled. "He came in on the supply truck, hidden in the back. He caught the guards by surprise when he leaped out of it. The sentries at the gates were alert, but those inside the camp didn't expect trouble."

"Wait," said Khatib. "What's this about the fence links being severed?"

Ahmad shrugged. "We found a section of the fence that was cut. I assumed that was how he got in."

Khatib said slowly, "I thought the fence was electrified."

"It has been," Ahmad answered, noting with apprehension the deepening glower on the face of his leader. "But the generator we have isn't powerful enough to supply current to the fence and also give us enough power to run our radio equipment. Up to two days ago, Khatib, the fence was charged. Then we turned on our transmitter for the first tests. We've been here for two months, and there's been no trouble. Who would have thought—"

"Fool!" Khatib exploded. "It's your responsibility to think! When you turned off the current to the fence, did you add more guards?"

Ahmad flushed, embarrassed, seething inside. "No. As I said—"

"I heard you once! Do you know what the cut in the fence means?"

"That someone entered secretly—"

Khatib cut him short. "Yes! Someone entered our camp secretly. And then this...this...dog sneaked in a second time in the back of a truck! We've had our security breached *twice!* Not just once! Twice! And you are responsible!" He whipped around to glare at Fuad.

"How many men have we lost, Fuad?"

"Eighteen," Fuad replied slowly. "And another seven are badly wounded."

"Twenty-five men!" Khatib was screaming now, spittle frothing at the corners of his mouth. "Twenty-five brethren because you didn't do your job the way you should have!"

"I was busy setting up the equipment," Ahmad defended himself. "There were others—"

"But I charged you with the responsibility!" the head Arab raged. "Twenty-five men! And Soraya!"

There was a silence as he threw her name at Ahmad. His henchman had no answer.

"Yes! Soraya! What's happened to her?"

Fuad held out his hands placatingly. Ahmad said nothing, but his dark face hardened.

Khatib ranted on. "No one knows! The last any of us saw of her, this...this mad dog had taken her with him! Soraya is his prisoner! That is," he snarled, "if she is still alive!"

Khatib spun away from them. Neither of them made a sound. They knew Khatib's insane rages. He was capable of whipping out a knife and slashing their throats when the blind fury of his anger took control of him.

Like a wild, caged lion, Khatib paced back and forth in the narrow confines of the room.

"He's rescued our prisoner—and he has Soraya," he muttered aloud, talking to himself. "So, most likely, he knows why we are here—and what we intend to do. Inshallah! It is fate!"

He took a deep breath, trying to control his rage.

"So be it! But nothing will stop us. At the appointed time, I will send the signal to change the orbit of the satellite!"

"If all goes well," Fuad murmured.

Khatib heard him. He strode over to the young man, seizing him by the front of his fatigues and pulling the terrorist close to him. He thrust his enraged face into that of the younger Arab. Close up, Fuad could see the hysterical madness burning in his leader's dark eyes. They blazed with a wild fanaticism.

"*Nothing* will stop me!" Khatib ranted. "Nothing! Do you hear me, Fuad? I have spent too much time putting this plan into operation! Two years! I will not be prevented from carrying it out! I will trigger the satellite signals myself this very morning!"

He thrust the young Arab away from him so violently that Fuad fell to his knees. He arose slowly.

Khatib turned on Ahmad.

"Do I hear a protest, Ahmad?"

The muscular Arab shook his head. A grin spread across his features.

"Not from me, my brother! I am with you completely. I would like to have my finger beside yours on the switch when it is pressed."

"In just a few hours," breathed Khatib. "I will show them!"

"In the name of the Prophet," Ahmad added. "*Ya aini,* upon my eyes, you are right! We will show them! It will be the beginning of the rule of Islam over the world!"

And then, spontaneously, they cried out, "*Allah! Allah akhbar!* Allah is great!"

# CHAPTER TWENTY-TWO

THE MARINE PILOT'S name was Koenig. He and Bolan dragged the unconscious body of the copilot into the shelter of the thatched hut. A thin trickle of blood from the guy's scalp was the only evidence that he was hurt.

Soraya pried open the copilot's eyelids and shone the flashlight into them. There was no reaction.

"Concussion?" asked Major Koenig.

The girl nodded. "It looks serious," she said. "He needs a doctor badly."

Koenig looked at Mack Bolan, and the big guy read the unasked question in the major's face. He shook his head.

"There's not a damn thing we can do for him here, major. Not even a first aid pack. Mine's been used up."

"But, dammit, he needs medical attention!"

"So do you," Bolan replied. "How's your arm?"

The major shrugged. "Hurts like hell. I think it's broken. I can't move it."

"Let me put it in a sling," Soraya volunteered. She helped the Marine out of his shirt and ripped off the sleeves, knotting them together.

Bolan stared bleakly out into the night and the rain, his mind on the problem that faced them.

With the force of the storm increasing as the hurricane approached, it didn't look as if they could count on any outside help.

So that left it up to him.

They couldn't stay where they were. Now it was not just Laconia whose life was at stake: the copilot was seriously hurt, too. Both of them would die if they didn't get medical treatment—and soon.

The big guy thought about the truck he had used in setting up his ambush of Spinney. For a moment, he wished he still had the damn thing. At least it would get them out of the mountains down to the port.

Yeah, but what good would that do? he asked himself. A jouncing ride of how many hours? How long could Laconia or the copilot take the punishment?

And if he got to Puerto Obaldía, then what? The coastal town lay directly in the path of the oncoming hurricane. There'd be no way to get the wounded men out of there.

Still, it would be better than nothing, wouldn't it?

All right, so the first truck was gone. Well, hell, he knew where he could find another.

Yeah. It meant another smash and grab, but this time with two objectives. First, to blow the hell out of the Intelsat antenna. Second, to steal one of their trucks!

Okay, so the mission had escalated way the hell beyond the original orders that Hal Brognola had given him what seemed a lifetime ago.

And, yeah, it meant another penetration of

the Arab camp. Back into that hornets' nest he'd stirred up with his last blitz—where every terrorist was armed and waiting, each one filled with a burning, vicious anger, aching to get revenge because the man in fighting black had humiliated them. He'd caused the deaths of their comrades, not only when he'd turned the hardsite into a blazing hellground, but also in his ambush of Spinney, when he'd wiped out every man of the escort!

Each of them would willingly die—if they could kill Mack Bolan.

And he was going to give them their chance.

There was no other way he could figure out—if he was going to achieve his twin objectives!

GRIMALDI HAD PICKED up the VORTAC station on Taboga Island as soon as he'd taken off from Howard. He'd set up his nav equipment, feeding in the omni range frequency and the radial he'd selected, and flicked on the DME, which kept him constantly informed about his exact distance from the station. He'd selected a compass radial out of the Taboga VORTAC that would take him past Isla del Rey in the Gulf of Panama, then across the Golfo de San Juan, to make a landfall just south of the La Palma VOR station.

The first of the storm winds hit him about the time he began his overland approach to the foothills of the mountain range.

The Bell Cobra was a lighter aircraft than the Sikorsky Sea Stallion. It pitched and bucked in the increasingly strong winds and erratic gusts.

Ahead of him, a cloud mass stretched ominously, low and threatening, all the way to the peaks of the mountains. Rain began pelting the cockpit Plexiglas.

Grimaldi flipped on the radio communications set when he was still 40 miles from the range, but he decided to wait until he crossed the crest of the mountains to begin his call-up. Bolan was still somewhere on the eastern slopes, and the land mass would block his VHF line-of-sight transmission.

When he was still 20 miles from the mountain foothills, the solid mass of the low clouds had forced him down to no more than 150 feet above the terrain. Wind gusts were lifting and dropping the light whirlybird 20 feet at a time. In the darkness, with rain lashing at the bubble canopy, he had no visibility at all. Without terrain radar, the flight would have been impossible.

Grimaldi took an exceptionally severe jolt and swore at himself. What kind of a damn fool was he to attempt something like this when the military had said it couldn't be done? And what kind of a damn fool was he to think he was a better pilot than the services had?

Or braver?

No, not braver. Just more of a gambler. More willing to take on greater risks. More willing to stick out his neck.

Because he was doing it for a buddy.

Every combat soldier knew that feeling. Knew that you'd take on crazy risks because the other guy was your buddy. Do things for him you'd never do for yourself.

Like die for him.

And Mack Bolan was his buddy. Friend. Leader.

He pushed on into the darkness and rain. . . .

# CHAPTER TWENTY-THREE

ONCE AGAIN, Bolan rigged for open warfare. The AutoMag .44 pistol and the 9mm Beretta Brigadier automatic with its tubular silencer screwed onto the end of the barrel had both been exposed to the rain.

Bolan field-stripped each of the guns in turn, wiping down every part with gun oil. Barrel, breech, slide mechanism, recoil springs, sear—the works. He reassembled the two handguns, checked the action for smoothness, oiled each cartridge, and reloaded the clips.

The Stoner was next. He stripped every cartridge from the spare ammo clips, loading them all into the 150-round drum magazine. Five thirty-round clips filled it.

After that, he took apart the two AK-47s. "AVTOMAT KALASHNIKOV MODIFICATION-NII" were what he had. The AK-47 was one of the best assault rifles used today. The Russians not only supplied them to their satellite countries, but helped many of the countries set up their own AK-47 manufacturing plants. Better than thirty-five million of these weapons had been turned out.

Firing a 7.62mm slug from a thirty-round, forward-curving clip at the rate of 800 a minute, it

was one hell of a rugged weapon. Of course, it had
its disadvantages, Bolan knew. One of the deadli-
est was that, unlike American automatic
weapons, it had no hold-open device to lock back
the bolt when the last round was fired. It just
stopped firing, so you had to kind of keep track of
how many rounds you thought you'd fired and
then slam in a fresh clip when the chatter quit on
you.

Bolan field-stripped the AK-47s, oiled them,
checked them as carefully as he had the others,
and then stripped, oiled, and reloaded each of the
spare ammo clips he'd picked up for them.

He counted his grenades, separating the frag
bombs from the flash bombs, pinching the ends of
the cotter key safety pins together so they'd come
out easily.

It took him more than an hour, even working
rapidly, to prepare his meager armament.

It wasn't much.

Not when he had to go up against at least two
dozen Arab hardmen. Sure, he'd taken half the
original number of them out of action—permanently! But that still left anywhere from twenty to
twenty-five of them, and. . .

The thought grew sickeningly in his mind: even
taking them on one or two at a time, the odds were
incredibly high against him!

And if there were more than one or two at a
time facing him—*and there would be*—then his
chances of survival were just about nil!

There had to be a way of cutting down the odds.
A way he could use his brains to outwit them.
Where his hard-won combat experience would

give him the edge, rather than go blitzing in on them in a frontal attack.

But there wasn't one.

It was going to have to be Bolan, all by his lonesome self, up against some two dozen hard, fanatical terrorists, armed with the same kind of AK-47s he'd just finished cleaning.

And who were, right now, waiting for him with revenge burning in their guts!

GRIMALDI TOOK the chopper through the mountain passes at a low level. Winds gusted, pounded at the light aircraft, because they were channeled through the narrow defiles. But he had no other choice. He couldn't go up into the solid cloud banks. Not with the limited navigational equipment in the Cobra. It wasn't designed for IFR flight.

His hands struggled with both control sticks; his feet played on the rudder pedals, and all the time, he had minimal forward visibility with the rain coming down heavily now to drench his bubble canopy.

The muscles of his forearms began to ache with the strain. He forced himself to ignore it, concentrating on battling his way through the hell of the growing storm. Sweat broke out on his forehead, and his shirt became drenched from the high humidity.

The chopper bounced erratically, lurching, staggering through the turbulence. More than once it exceeded its strain limits, but it managed to come through. Grimaldi tried not to think about the incredible pressures twisting the rotor blades.

Three quarters of an hour later, he broke through to the eastern slopes of the range. The wind was stronger on the Caribbean side of the foothills because of the approaching storm center. The Cobra slammed its way across the sky as Grimaldi took a northerly course.

Now he flicked on his VHF transmitter and began his call up.

"Stony Man One... Stony Man One.... This is Stony Man Two.... Come in, Stony Man One...."

Again and again, he broadcast his appeal for Mack Bolan to answer him.

THE ONLY INDICATION that dawn had arrived was a lightening of the sky to the east, and then the dark gave way to a gray overcast.

Mack Bolan stepped outside the hut, carrying the reloaded Stoner and wearing his backpack. Behind him, in the doorway, Major Koenig and the girl, Soraya, watched him go without saying a word. There was nothing to say, once he'd explained why he had to make the attempt.

"I wish to hell I was going with you," the Marine had said, angrily.

The big guy was almost to the far edge of the clearing when the high-pitched *beep-beep* of his radio alerted him. Flipping it from his belt, Bolan snapped it on.

"...Man One.... Come in, Stony Man One...."

For a moment, Bolan couldn't believe he was hearing the voice.

"This is G Boy.... Come in, Stony Man One...."

Yeah! G Boy! Jack Grimaldi! And Bolan didn't

need the code name identification for him to recognize the hotshot pilot's voice.

Bolan grinned. A big, wide, mouth-splitting grin.

"This is Stony Man One," he said crisply into the mike. "I read you, G Boy.... What the hell are you doing here?"

The reply crackled back at him.

*"Just happened to be in the neighborhood.... Thought I'd drop in and say hello.... Turn on your porchlight so I can find you...."*

Bolan's grin turned into a chuckle. Turn on the porchlight, huh? Homing beacon was more like it! He slipped his backpack off and dug into it.

Once more, he set up the small black locator transmitter and flipped it on.

His walkie-talkie erupted. *"Loud and clear... Stony Man One.... Be with you in five minutes."*

It was only three minutes, though, before Bolan heard the snarling buzz of a jet turbine engine mixed with the angry *whup-whap* of rotor blades slapping apart the rain-filled sky. And then the mean, deadly lines of the olive-drab-painted fighter helicopter screamed into view.

It slid toward him, crabbing at an angle, hovered over him for the briefest moment, and then set itself down smoothly on its pipe skids.

Grimaldi ducked out of the cockpit as the turbine whined down and the rotor blades slowed. Bolan came to meet him.

"What the hell are you doing here?" he demanded a second time.

Grimaldi lifted an innocent face toward him.

"They tell me it's kind of hard to find a taxi down here," he answered with a straight face, but his eyes crinkled with amusement. "You want a ride home, boss?"

Bolan didn't respond to Grimaldi's humor.

"I've got three wounded men back in that hut," he said tersely. "Two of them are unconscious: the third has a broken arm. And there's a girl, too."

Grimaldi's eyebrows lifted.

"Can you fit us all into that chopper?"

Grimaldi shook his head. "No way, Sarge. It's not the weight. I can carry a hell of a lot more than all of you combined. It's the space. I've got room for a gunner. That's it. And it's getting rough out there. What were you going to do if I hadn't come along?"

Bolan sketched out his plans. Grimaldi whistled. "Hey! A guy can get himself killed that way."

"The odds aren't the same anymore," Bolan replied. "Not with you and that chopper—"

"And the goodies I brought along," Grimaldi cut in. "Like a wire-guided antitank missile launcher and a case of rocket ammo for it. That suit you?"

Bolan grinned. "Yeah."

"And the Cobra is fully armed. Pods loaded with air-to-ground missiles. Now, can you brief me on the layout of the hardsite?"

Squatting on the ground of the clearing, Bolan scratched a rough map of the enemy camp and its buildings into the mud.

Grimaldi studied it intently.

Major Koenig came across the field. Grimaldi looked up as the man approached.

Bolan introduced them.

"This is Major Koenig. Major—Jack Grimaldi."

The Marine looked at Grimaldi and then at the Cobra. Grimaldi wore no uniform.

As they shook hands, left-handed, Koenig remarked, "I guess I better not ask what service you're in, huh?"

Whatever reply Grimaldi might have made was cut off. Bolan's radio beeper sounded its shrill cry one more time.

And then, before he could answer, the three men heard the distinctive air-slap of helicopter blades.

Grimaldi whipped around, scanning the skies. Bolan caught sight of it first—coming in from the west.

"There!"

Grimaldi started to race for the Cobra. Only Major Koenig's shout stopped him.

"Hold it, man! It's one of ours!"

Grimaldi halted, his eyes fixed on the bird as it raced over the clearing to set down less than 30 feet from his own chopper.

The big Sea Stallion dwarfed the Cobra.

The instant its skids touched, men began pouring from it.

"Medivac!" shouted the Marine. "Goddamn the beautiful bastards! I knew they wouldn't abandon us!"

A chunky captain ran up to them, saluting.

Koenig pointed to the thatch hut. "In there. Two badly wounded men."

The Marine officer spun around, shouting at his corpsmen. Stretchers came out of the belly of the chopper. Men raced with them to the hut. Soraya came out.

In minutes, the blanket-wrapped form of Laconia was brought out, followed by that of the Marine copilot.

Soraya came over to Mack Bolan and Jack Grimaldi. Grimaldi eyeballed her from head to toe.

Bolan said, "Major Koenig, I guess you're in charge. It's imperative that that man—" he pointed to Laconia as his stretcher was being loaded aboard the Sea Stallion "—gets to Washington as soon as possible. He's to be flown on through."

The Marine acknowledged the order with a quick salute. He turned to the girl.

"Let's go, miss," he said. "They're ready for takeoff."

Soraya hesitated, as if reluctant to leave. She looked pleadingly at Bolan.

"You must go with them now," he commanded. "It's your only chance."

There would be no disobeying the tone of command in Bolan's voice. Koeing and the girl ran toward the chopper. Even as they climbed aboard, the cargo compartment doors slammed shut, and the big machine rose into the air. It spun in a half-circle and raced off into the murky sky.

Bolan touched Grimaldi's arm, and squatted down over the rough sketch he'd drawn in the dirt.

"Now," he began, "here's what we do. . . ."

# CHAPTER TWENTY-FOUR

WITH BOLAN IN THE GUNNER'S SEAT ahead of and below him in the slim fuselage, Jack Grimaldi took the Cobra off the ground, circled once in the rain to orient himself, and then, following Bolan's directions in his earphones, set off toward the terrorist hardsite. Irregular showers slashed at his cockpit Plexiglas.

Flying so low that he barely cleared the tree-tops, crabbing into the wind at an angle against the growing force of the approaching storm, the ex-Vietnam pilot slid the bird across the terrain to intersect the mountain road, about a mile and a half away.

He crossed over the evidence of Bolan's earlier firefight, the forward speed of the Cobra down to only a few miles an hour. Looking down on the smashed truck that still lay across the roadbed, he noticed there were no bodies in view.

And then he was past the truck, letting the helicopter sink even lower so that it was flying just above the channels cut in the gravel by the rain.

Bolan lifted his arm and pointed.

"About a hundred yards farther up," he said over the intercom. "You can set me down there."

Grimaldi touched down the pipe skids on the rain-soaked roadway.

With the Cobra's rotors still whirling overhead, the big man with the ice-blue eyes scrambled out of the machine. His backpack, now loaded with rocket missiles, came out next, and then he hauled the slim, lightweight, wire-guided antitank launcher out of the main cabin, along with its power pack/computer box.

Grimaldi grinned down at him. Over the roar of the idling turbine engine, he shouted, "Give 'em hell, Sarge!"

Bolan flashed his own grin back at Grimaldi. He tapped the flare pistol Grimaldi had brought him, which was now hooked to his web belt.

"Ten minutes!" he shouted back. "Then watch for the flare! You should be able to see it from here!"

Grimaldi held up his right hand in a "four-oh!" signal—forefinger and thumb touching and the other three fingers erect and spread.

And then Bolan was out from under the whipping blades of the chopper with his war baggage, slipping into his backpack. The M63A1 Stoner with its 150-round drum was in his right hand; the AK-47 was slung over his shoulder.

For a moment he stood there, a hard, powerful figure in his skin-tight black combat suit, impervious to the rain falling on him, the epitome of the battle-ready fighting man set to move into action.

He made one last adjustment to the pack straps and, without another sign to Grimaldi, turned on his heel and started up the road, breaking into a jogging trot in his first few strides. In seconds, he had disappeared into the rain and fog.

Phantasmal echoes of earlier conflicts mingled with the air currents from the jungle floor to tickle his mind with their implications of war everlasting. Had there ever been a time when men were not called upon to lay down their dreams and pick up the weapons of war in defense of the human estate?

What is that estate? Is it worth the price? Is war the only viable alternative?

War everlasting? Probably, yeah. That war had begun, no doubt, in a jungle very like this one. And it had marked the beginning of the human race.

Farfetched? Maybe not. Man is a warlike creature because he was produced by warfare, born to the task, forever locked in the titanic struggle to maintain that separation of the species.

Man: captain of his own fate, protector of his own identity. Man: master of the earth, created by the exigencies of survival, born into his own mind and spirit by the simple act of standing up and striking back—the hunted becoming the hunter, the weak transformed into the strong by the simple decision to stand and fight.

Warrior Man had to fight for the luxury of contemplating a better life. At what point had it become a "right"—the right to life, the right to liberty, the right to pursue happiness? There were no such rights for primeval man. Was the first act of war also the first declaration of human rights? Probably. But the war had never been won, the "rights" never firmly established. Very likely they never would be. Warfare seems to be a human need, forever interwoven into that complex structure that has become indentified as Man.

The idea of "rights" is entirely a human idea. It is a conception of a complicated mind—and had it not been the cause of warfare then it was, at least, the inevitable consequence. The real war, the true war, had nothing to do with tribal boundaries or clan loyalties. The eternal war, *necessary* war, was Man determined to be Man: Man the Savage struggling continually to become Man the Noble. A paradox, sure. But the war goes on.

There was a time when this warrior dreamed of peace. He no longer does that. Peace is an abstract, a dalliance of the mind, a retreat from the reality that was Life. A fantasy. Life for Man—true life—is a continuing process of self-identification—and that always means war, of one sort or another.

Bolan had come to accept it, to reconcile himself to the reality. Man was the Noble Savage. A Romantic. Man imagined that he could make a perfect world. He had been trying to do so since the beginning of his time. This noble quest had provided his identity in a world immersed in the struggle for survival. Romantic Man, the Noble Savage, entertaining the intimations of a nobler world.

Even as he went to war....

# CHAPTER TWENTY-FIVE

BOLAN LAY PRONE at the edge of the clearing that ran around the Arab hardsite, ignoring the wet ground and the discomfort, ignoring the rain, too. His powerful binoculars pulled him in through the mist to a front seat in the enemy camp.

He'd wanted to get behind the camp, where he could have a clear shot down at the base of the transmitting antenna, but now the camp was alerted, and there were hardmen patrolling the far slope.

Four sentries were on duty at the gate. Elsewhere, they patrolled in pairs. Over by the barracks shack, drivers sat in the cabs of two trucks, the engines running, and Bolan knew that at the first sign of trouble, armed terrorists would erupt out of the barracks to pile into the trucks and race to the hot spot.

Okay. Surveillance completed. Nothing to change the basic tactical plan he'd worked out with Grimaldi.

In his mind, the countdown to hell began ticking off.

Bolan squirmed back a few feet and began to set up the launcher system. Still prone under the cover of the scrub brush, but with a clear field of fire in front of him, he connected the power box/computer control system with the launching tube. He snapped the optical sight into place, pushed home the electrical connections, and put the eyepiece to his face.

Cross hairs centered. The image was big and sharp.

The first wire-guided rocket went into the launcher. Grimaldi had brought him five rockets. He set the remaining four in front of him in a row.

Targets One and Two were the trucks waiting with their engines running in front of the barracks.

Target Three was the headquarters shack.

Target Four was the concrete-block building housing the computers.

And Target Five would be the dish antenna—*if* he could get into the camp for a clear shot at it!

But he would not blast those Scud missiles. A hit on the headquarters shack and the computer base would wipe out any chance of a launch—you unplug a missile system and nothing in the world will get them off the ground.

But a stray rocket into that bed of primed death and the whole mountain could go up. That would be overkill—an end not only to Khatib's terrorists, but to Soraya, Laconia, Grimaldi and the chopper, and Bolan, too. He must avoid the Scuds, and by as wide a margin as possible! Otherwise it was a trip to the top of the sky, with no ticket back.

He took a practice aim at each target in turn, selecting the exact spot he wanted the high explosive shell to slam into, memorizing the picture he saw through the sights and filing it away in his mind.

The Stoner lay alongside his right leg, partially sheltered from the rain by his body. The Kalashnikov lay next to it.

He took out the flare pistol, broke it open, loaded a fat flare cartridge into it, snapped it shut, and cocked it. He set it on the ground in front of him, then picked up the launch tube, and set it firmly into his shoulder, the padded rim of the eyepiece hard against the bone of his forehead and cheek.

Now! His finger stroked the trigger.

Hell blazed out of the muzzle of the launcher, streaming a thin trail of smoke across the distance between Bolan and the lead truck.

Immediately, he picked up the Stoner and loosed off a couple of short, aimed bursts at the four guards at the gate area, catching them as they spun around in surprise.

The 5.56mm tumblers stitched a path across their guts, doubling them over. Even as they fell, he followed them in his sights, sending another couple of bursts slamming into their bodies, the slugs blasting apart skull bones and brain in a long-distance *coup de grâce*.

Now he put down the Stoner and picked up the flare gun. He raised his hand and arm straight overhead as he pulled the trigger. The flare whipped into the sky, arching as it soared upward to burst in a pattern of crimson. He knew that Grimaldi was watching for it, and that the idling turbines of the Cobra would be revving up and the great rotor blades would be slashing the air faster and faster, building up lift that would carry the hellship into battle.

In the enemy camp, chaos broke loose. The deep, hard blast of the exploding rocket missile that had destroyed the lead truck echoed through the hardsite, followed immediately by the rapid-fire *chit-chit-chit-chit* of the M63A1 on full automatic.

Bodies piled out of the barracks hut as the hardmen scrambled in a rush for the trucks. It was what the big guy had planned for.

The launcher tube went up to his shoulder again. Cross hairs centered on the second truck. He eased the trigger and followed the smoke trail through the magnified view in the optical sight, keeping the hairs aligned. The hell bomb whipped into the truck cab through the windshield, blasting its way into the truck body now filled with armed terrorists.

The truck blew apart.

Hell, it ought to. The wire-guided missiles were designed to punch their way through the inches-thick hardened steel plating of a tank turret! This was like smashing sardine tins with an axe!

Chunks of steel ripped apart, spinning through the air. Shreds of bloody flesh splatted against the wall of the shack. The gas tank blew. A sheet of orange red flame soared skyward to scorch the human meat in midflight.

Bolan had kept his promise. He had turned the terrorist hardsite into a hellground of terror.

Yeah, now it was their turn to experience the shock and panic and paralyzing horror they'd meted out to others—only the others were innocents and they weren't. They deserved everything he was handing out to them.

And he wasn't through yet!

He switched to Target Three—and watched grimly as the rocket exploded viciously into the headquarters shack.

Hardmen boiled out of the remaining huts. Sentries on duty around the perimeter of the campsite came running.

Target Four coming up—the concrete-block electronics shack.

And then he eased his finger off the trigger as he swore out loud.

Tearing in from his right, coming in out of the mist and rain, preceded by the whining scream of a turbine at full throttle and the flat, furious *blat-blat-blat* of rotor blades, the deadly sleekness of the olive-drab Cobra whipped into view, slashing across the hardsite with its turreted Mini-gun blazing away, cutting a lethal path across the center of the camp.

Bolan didn't dare fire the launcher. Whatever he hit could throw up debris that might smash a rotor blade.

For a moment, in pure enjoyment, he watched a master fighter pilot at work as Grimaldi spun and danced the attack helicopter through the air over the Arab encampment. Slipping, skidding, hovering for a moment in one spot while he rotated the body of the chopper in a circle, the Mini-gun blasting away, Grimaldi slung a deadly hail of lead at whatever targets of opportunity he could find.

All around the hardsite, terrorists running in a crouch were suddenly jerked upright, only to collapse as the lead stingers ripped them apart, tearing tissue and flesh and bone in eruptions of blood.

Bolan grabbed at the Stoner. He caught sight of one Arab who, driven into a fury, suddenly leaped erect, and was aiming his AK-47 at the chopper.

He gave the hardman no time to fire. Mini-slugs from the Stoner cut him down as Bolan stroked the trigger.

Now the hellship screamed up and slanted off, out of the fray. It was Mack Bolan's turn once again.

Incredibly, a third truck appeared, unharmed, from behind tree cover at the rear of the camp. As Bolan watched in alarm, the driver threw it in gear, and it began to lurch away from the barracks hut to speed toward the gate in a surprise effort to come to grips with the enemy attacking them frontally.

Bolan estimated there had to be ten to twelve of the Arab hardmen in this truck he had not accounted for. Too many to confront head on.

He picked up the missile launcher, caught the speeding vehicle in the cross hairs of the optical sight, centered them, and loosed off an armor-piercing round.

The speeding truck had to swerve around the bodies littering the hardsite. Bolan kept the cross hairs of the launch tube's sight locked onto the body of the vehicle, and the computer guts in the power-control box did the rest.

Trailing its thin filament of wire, the missile blasted toward the truck, turning and swerving to follow every movement it made, its flight controlled by electric impulses it received from the black box.

The armor-piercing, high-explosive shell impacted into the truck chassis just behind the cab.

Even through the blast, Bolan could see the truck slam over onto its side: the optical sight brought him right into the action. Ripped bodies hurtled into the air. What was left of the truck rolled over twice, burning furiously.

Bolan leaped up.

Green flare into the sky.

And the Cobra slashed back into action to provide covering fire for the big guy with the ice-blue eyes as he ran across the clearing toward the hardsite.

Carrying the Stoner at the ready, Bolan trotted past the dead sentries at the gate.

He cut around behind the headquarters building, keeping to the right side of the hardsite, while Grimaldi poured fire in on the terrorist hardmen from the chopper overhead.

# CHAPTER TWENTY-SIX

WHEN THE FIRST HARD BLAST of the explosion rocked the hardsite, Khatib al Sulieman was in his headquarters shack, pacing impatiently back and forth, waiting with Fuad for word that Ahmad had completed testing the system so that it could be triggered.

Like the others, they ran outside, in time to see the destruction of the truck filled with his men as Bolan sent a rocket missile into it.

And then all hell broke loose.

Out of the rain clouds, behind its own storm of lead slugs from the turreted Mini-gun, the sleek, lethal attack helicopter arrowed in to turn the hardsite into the devil's playground. Men fell in their tracks. Others dove headlong for whatever shelter they could find.

Khatib raced for the equipment shack, only to throw himself to the ground as the chopper roared hellishly overhead. Desperately, he crawled behind the false protection of a shack to wait out the attack. The instant the chopper withdrew, Khatib was on his feet, running for the control shack, followed by a terrified Fuad.

He burst in the door, streaming from the rain, to carom into Ahmad Mashir. The terrorist had an AK-47 in his hand. Blood madness glared out of his crazed eyes.

Khatib grabbed him.

"Where do you think you're going?"

"To launch the missiles!"

Khatib tore the assault rifle from his hench-man's grip. "Fool! I need you here! How soon can we trigger the signals to destroy the satellite?"

Ahmad fought against his grip. "Give me back my weapon!"

Khatib slapped him across the face with the flat of his hand. "You can do nothing out there! Answer my question!"

Fuad answered for him.

"Twenty minutes. Can we hold them off that long?"

"No! Can it be done faster?"

Khatib shoved the stocky figure of Ahmad away from him. He strode over to Fuad.

"*Can it be done faster?*" he screamed.

"No. The satellite will not be in position."

Khatib hesitated a second. He made up his mind.

"Trigger it anyhow! As soon as you can!"

Fuad shrugged and turned back to the equipment. Khatib turned to speak to Ahmad, but he was gone.

So was the AK-47.

The lust for battle had proven too strong for the fanatical revolutionary. Nothing could keep him from the battle raging outside.

THE WAY WASN'T EASY for the Executioner. There were even more hardmen than he'd counted.

Two of them popped up on his right as he jogged in through the gates. Bolan caught their images in his peripheral vision. Without conscious thought his hands snapped the Stoner around, loosing off a sustained burst that cut them down.

From ahead and to his left came the heavier chatter of an AK-47, but the death specialist was already moving in a tumbling dive to his right, landing in a skidding roll that brought him back up on one knee in the mud to answer the challenge with a hard burst of his own.

Through the mist of rain, he saw the muzzle of an assault rifle poking its way out the window of a hut. Bolan's hand was a blur as he yanked a frag grenade out of the pouch on his belt, snapped out the pin, and flung the grenade in through the window opening.

He was around the corner of another hut and running hard when it blew the shack apart.

He had his target in sight now.

The concrete-block building that housed the computers.

Destroy them, and the dish-shaped antenna would be silenced.

But it was not to be—not just then.

The stocky figure of a terrorist, an AK-47 in both hands and the wild, insane glare of battle in his eyes, came charging out.

The Stoner fired off one round—and the bolt locked open and empty.

In that fraction of a microsecond, Bolan's brain registered the sound and he reacted.

His right hand slapped the butt of the AutoMag on his hip. The heavy silver automatic pistol leaped into his palm, its muzzle jerking up, and a solid 240 grains of jacketed lead roared from the muzzle to blast its way through the chest wall of the maddened Yemeni.

The reflex tightening of Ahmad's finger brought a responsive burst from the AK-47, but it was too late.

The slugs spun howling into the air as his dead body was slammed backward by the enormous foot-pounds of energy carried by the heavy slug.

And now the enemy fire sought Bolan out. He dove for the protection of the concrete-block walls. The flaregun came out of his belt. He fired it into the looming clouds. And the lean, olive-drab machine that was the Cobra came hurtling out of the rain to rake the area with its Mini-gun, driving the Arab hardmen into cover. It roared in to make an impossible landing in the space in front of the equipment shack.

Bolan was on his feet, diving for the door of the chopper. Grimaldi leaned out the cockpit window, screaming at him.

The man in black wrenched open the door to the gunner's seat, gesturing with his hand as he dove in, and Grimaldi had the deadly whirlybird clawing for the sky even before Bolan was fully inside.

The Cobra rose only a few feet before Grimaldi threw it into backward flight, withdrawing in a circular flight path behind the protection of the concrete-block shelter and the hail of lead minislugs from the belly turret of the Cobra.

And then he spun it into an upward spiral that took it out of the firefight into the safety of the low-lying clouds.

# CHAPTER TWENTY-SEVEN

WINDS LASHED AT THE BODY of the Cobra as Grimaldi took it away from the plateau and the hardsite, leaving behind the bodies of the dead and wounded terrorists.

Bolan had more than decimated their forces. To decimate is to kill one out of every ten. And the big guy with the ice-blue eyes and the cold hatred in his heart for the callous terrorists who killed indiscriminately and mercilessly had done away with a hell of a lot more than one out of every ten of the Arab hardmen.

In fact, if someone had counted the numbers, the ratio would have been the other way around! Fewer than one in ten were still alive!

Grimaldi flicked on his intercom.

"Home, boss?" he asked, already beginning to edge the chopper into a course that would skirt low over the ground, planning in his mind the route that would take them through the valleys and out of the storm.

He was startled by Bolan's reply.

"Back to the hardsite," came the tough rejoinder. "We haven't finished the job."

BACK AT THE ARAB CAMP, rain fell on the dead, washing the blood from their wounds into the ground. Stunned terrorists gathered to count the living and to assess the damage inflicted on them.

After the fury of the battle, the comparative quiet was strange, broken only by the moans of the wounded and the falling raindrops.

Mohammed Shahadeh was crossing the compound when he stopped, his ears picking up a faint noise. It took him only a second to identify it.

He broke into a run, shouting at the top of his lungs.

"They are coming again! Brothers! They are coming again!"

BOLAN THUMBED the intercom switch.

"Target One is the antenna. Target Two is the concrete-block building that houses the control equipment. Got it?"

"Roger." Grimaldi's answer was crisp.

"We stay with Target One until it's destroyed completely."

Again the ex-Vietnam pilot acknowledged.

In the gunner's cockpit, ahead of and below the pilot, Mack Bolan's hard eyes narrowed, trying to peer through the distortion the raindrops made on the curved Plexiglas in front of him.

IN THE EQUIPMENT SHACK, Fuad's face streamed with sweat. The Arab bossman leaned over his shoulder, urging him to work faster.

"It is done! It is done!" Fuad protested. "I need only one last check. Give me thirty seconds!"

He lifted his face, his eyes shining with excitement. "And then you can trigger the signals yourself, my brother!"

BOLAN CROUCHED in the confines of the gunner's seat, ahead of and below Jack Grimaldi, his hands already on the Mini-gun turret controls and firing button.

Behind him, in the narrow stricture of the chopper cockpit, Grimaldi's hands were tense on the controls. The cyclic stick was in his right hand, the collective in his left. His feet played on the "rudder" pedals that controlled the speed of the tail rotor.

From time to time, his eyes flicked to the instrument panel, scanning it at a glance, reading every instrument.

Rotor blade and engine tachs were in the green.

He pulled up on the collective with his left hand, increasing the whirlybird's speed and, simultaneously, made compensating motions with his other hand and his feet.

The angle of the helicopter body changed. The nose pointed down.

It came screaming out of the rain mists to attack the Arab compound like a giant, prehistoric bird, but there was fire and lightning in its beak and talons.

"NOW!" CRIED FUAD, slipping out of his seat. "Now we are ready!"

Khatib al Sulieman thrust his henchman out of his way. He sat down in front of the console. "Show me!"

Fuad leaned over his shoulder. "This is the sequence." He spoke rapidly, the words tumbling out of his mouth. His fingers flashed across the keyboard. "These keys. This one first. There will be a sequence on the screen. Then this one. The sequence will change. And then, finally, this key. When you press this key, you will—"

Khatib cut him off angrily. "I know!"

His finger pressed down on Key One.

"Now, Fuad, you can do what you like with Spinney's missiles. Point them at the Canal for all I care! My destiny is accomplished here. I am going to be the first to destroy a satellite. . . ."

As THEY CAME slanting across the clearing in front of the terrorist camp, Bolan picked up running figures in his gunsight.

Vibration from the rotor blades shook him in his seat. The roar of the jet turbine engine was continuous, and the hard, whacking pound of the blades slashing the air slammed at his ears.

Targets: a hardguy, on one knee, his assault rifle at his shoulder, firing up at them. Two of them near a shack, one kneeling, the other standing in the doorway. Both firing at the chopper. At Bolan. To the left, a group of four, three of them firing. The fourth brandishing his rifle overhead, his face contorted, his mouth opening to scream hysterical defiance at them.

Bolan's thumb pressed the remote trigger switch, and he spun the Mini-gun turret, and the sights cross-haired on his targets. The Mini-gun, slung under the nose of the Cobra, responded.

It was like having a lethal hose in his hands. Only instead of water, lead slugs poured from its muzzles in a stream of tumblers cutting down his targets.

Bodies sprawled and fell as the man in the

black fighting suit brought retribution and revenge back for a repeat performance.

A sermon in death!

Yeah, that's what it was. The rain of fire had obliterated the henchman Fuad only yards from the headquarters shack, and only seconds from his plan to launch the destruction of the Panama Canal. Fuad's stomach and intestines were gruesomely separated from the rest of him; his blood drenched the ground where he lay.

Bolan and Grimaldi blitzed past the falling bodies. Ahead of them, the huge, dish-shaped antenna loomed up.

Grimaldi had been holding the red asterisk sight of the Target Acquisition Pulse Monitor in his face mask on the antenna.

Bolan cracked, "Now!" into his mike.

And Grimaldi touched the trigger. Two air-to-ground missiles screamed out of the right-hand pod, their monitoring electronics locked in sync pulse with the asterisk sight in Grimaldi's helmet faceplate.

Red flash and smoke streamed past Bolan in his gunner's seat, the rockets trailing a thin plume as they flashed ahead of the attack chopper.

IN THE EQUIPMENT SHACK, sitting hunched over the computer console, Khatib al Sulieman's figure pressed the second button in the sequence and moved to hover over Key Three.

THE FIRST PAIR of rockets tore through the wire of the antenna. Grimaldi slid the helicopter in a tight turn, the body spinning around faster than the rotor blade angle to line up again with the target from a new attack approach.

"Target the base," Bolan snapped into his mike. Grimaldi dropped the nose of the Cobra down a couple of degrees and centered the red target sight in his faceplate on the antenna foundation.

Once more, a set of screaming air-to-ground missiles rocketed ahead of the helicopter.

THE MONITOR SCREEN in front of Khatib flicked into a new sequence of numbers. With a cry of exultation, the Palestinian bossman jabbed his forefinger down on the plastic key.

THE TWO ROCKETS slammed into the base of the antenna, exploding in a fiery burst that blew the dish apart, destroying the concrete base, the antenna mount, gears, power lines, and wiring.

THE SCREEN Khatib was staring at went blank, even as the Arab bossman's finger touched the plastic key. The cry of exultation died in his throat.

He stared at the blank screen.

In that second, because sound travels slower than impulses in microelectronic circuitry, the blast of the rockets destroying the dish antenna reached his ears.

The Palestinian knew immediately what had happened.

With a cry of rage, he rose from his seat, smashing his fist at the screen in frustration, and then spun around to race out the door.

His hand snatched up Fuad's AK-47 as he ran outside.

"TARGET TWO?" asked Grimaldi.

"Right," Bolan's voice cracked back. "Target Two."

The chopper skittered back across the camp, Bolan picking off another group of terrorists with the Mini-gun as Grimaldi made his run.

Bolan saw a figure dressed in fatigues tear out the door of the equipment shack.

He sighted in on him, fired, missed. And then he switched to the rocket armament.

His thumb stroked the trigger. Twin rockets— this time from the pod under the left wing stub— blasted into it. The figure was obliterated, lost in the blast as the concrete blocks of the shack disintegrated.

The helicopter peeled away in a sharp turn.

"Time to go home, boss?" Grimaldi asked the question a second time.

Bolan grinned, even though the pilot couldn't see it.

"Yeah. Time to go home."

## CHAPTER TWENTY-EIGHT

"WE GOT OUT just ahead of the hurricane," Bolan said easily. He leaned back in his armchair in the War Room at Stony Man Farm. "Grimaldi got us back to Howard, and wouldn't you know, Soraya was there, waiting."

They were gathered around him: Hal Brognola, who was conducting the debriefing for the man in the Oval Office; Rosario Blancanales; Gadgets Schwartz; Leo Turrin; and April Rose, who sat next to Mack Bolan, touching his arm from time to time.

Brognola said, "I got word this morning that Laconia's been moved to Walter Reed. The docs say he'll recover."

"Good. He went through hell."

The big federal agent had a final question. "Where the hell is Jack Grimaldi now?"

"Damned if I know," Bolan replied. "I left him and that Arab girl back in the Canal Zone when I got your message to head on home fast."

April cleared her throat. The tall, good-looking girl had a smile on her face.

"Maybe this will clear up the matter." She held out a cablegram to the fed agent. "It's from Jack Grimaldi in a resort hotel on the Caribbean coast of Mexico. He *says* he's on R & R! Indeed...."

When the laughter had died down, Bolan leaned forward and asked, "Hal, what was the rush about getting back here to Stony Man Farm?"

Brognola got to his feet. He put a large manila file folder on the desk in front of the wall screen.

"Striker," he said, "you know anything about Turkey—and present-day Armenian freedom groups?"

Bolan's ice-blue eyes sharpened the moment he heard the federal agent call him "Striker."

"You here to brief me on another mission, Hal?"

The federal agent nodded.

"Yeah. And there's not much time...."

**THE PRESIDENT**

HB — Suggest you now talk to Stony Man people about problem brewing in Turkish - Armenian sectors. This best handled unofficially, as per your SOP, as discussed. You may release all relevant data and resources as required.

OPERATIONAL IMMEDIATE

FR WHITE HOUSE/BROGNOLA 121310Z

TO STONYMAN ONE ·

BT

MISSION ALERT X

EXERCISE FULL PREROGATIVES X

TOPMAN REQUESTS X

RE ANKARA CONNECTION X

REGENT REPEAT REGENT NOW KNOWN OPERATING

WITHIN CONUS POSSIBLE PROVOCATION

TURKO-ARMENIAN SITUATION X ADAMIAN REPEAT

ADAMIAN DEFINITELY INVOLVED AND HEAVILY

COMMITTED X NSC CONCERNED RE USA-USSR

IMPLICATIONS IN CONTEXT USORGCRIME LINK X

REQUEST ALL DELICACY X FULL

LOGISTICS/RESOURCES AT YOUR COMPLETE

DISPOSAL X DATA PACKAGE FOLLOWS

BT

121310Z EOM

OPERATIONAL IMMEDIATE

FR STONYMAN OPS 121430Z

TO BROGNOLA/WH/WASHDC

BT

APRIL SENDS X SLATE STONYMAN REACTION RE

ANKARA CONNECTION X ABLE TEAM CONFIRMS

REGENT/ADAMIAN/ORGCRIME ANGLE X PHOENIX NOW

ENROUTE LAX TO INTERDICT UNHOLY ALLIANCE AND

HOPEFULLY RESOLVE SITUATION LOCALLY X THAT

FAILING PHOENIX PLANS TURKISH OPERATION AND

REQUESTS LEVEL ONE SUPPORT THAT AREA X

PLEASE CONFIRM SUPPORT LEVEL AND ARRANGE ALL

AIRLIFT REQUIREMENTS

BT

121430Z EOM

# MACK BOLAN

THE EXECUTIONER 40

## appears again in
## Double Crossfire

A brutal machine-gun fusillade in Beverly Hills opens this new Mack Bolan adventure, a story of combat, courage and political double-cross in the wild, uncharted terrain of Turkey.

No matter whether the enemy is Mafia, mugger or mercenary, Mack Bolan is sworn to avenge the corruption spread by all forces of darkness. His target is wherever in the world blind hatred has been unleashed. If the challenge is dangerous enough, Bolan will meet it, with actions that are lean, mean and swift.

News of a Washington diplomat's kidnap and incarceration overseas gives a new dimension to Bolan's latest mission. Backed by the resources of Stony Man Farm and the invincible Able Team, he leaps directly into the battleground. Bolan finds that the age-old conflict between the Turks and Armenians is being cruelly used as a cover. Long-smoldering hatred, the result of the hideous genocidal holocaust of 1915-18 when more than a million Armenians were killed, was now being exploited by fanatical terrorists. It is a scene of violent action in a strange and forbidding setting, and the No. 1 enemy is a mysterious Mafia-opium connection called Regent.

Regent is the kind of terrorist who has come from rags to ill-gotten riches...and now wants more. He and his ruthless sidekicks are enslaved by greed as completely as their victims are enslaved by opium. They are the kind of insidious human virus upon which Mack Bolan rains his brand of hellfire. There is literally no stopping Bolan's deadly dreadnought.

As always, Bolan approached the assignment on full alert.

He fed a can into the grenade launcher, to be held in readiness. He counted off fifteen beats, then stepped calmly into the open, strolling toward the meandering mountain stream that divided him from the dozen troops advancing in formation, rifles at the ready.

There was a shout, but the cry was cut off by the chatter of Bolan's M16. He had picked a man in the center of the approaching line and zipped him from head to toe in a burst of six shots. Then Bolan cut down the second man, then the third, the fourth....

These were soldiers who had struck an unholy alliance with international street crime. It was incredible how in their desperation and feverish greed for blood and gold, Regent's hardmen had sold themselves utterly to the drug syndicates that were crippling so many in the free world. And, yeah, they had sold themselves to the unremitting bloodletting of this battlefield. They had become targets for Bolan's swiftness and strength. And even though they vastly outnumbered him, they hardly had a chance.

*Bolan triggered the launcher. The grenade blast engulfed the troops, pinning them down in a gray-white smoke. Some of them staggered out of it.*

*One of the foot soldiers was desperately trying to unjam his rifle, his head down, working furiously. Another soldier nearby was looking up, his eyes deep pools of shock and horror. For the big man in black was about to give the two of them a fast figure-eight burst from the M16.*

*Paralyzed, they stared down the rifle barrel, recognizing the gaping hole of death. In split seconds, neither of them would be there anymore.*

*A grim revelation. Yeah, final revelation.*

Mack's enemies in *Double Crossfire* bring out the best in a warrior who has been tested by the most powerful and deadly forces of evil during his many years as the Executioner. If Mack Bolan cannot bend heaven, he will move hell. It is a philosophy that, at every turn, has won him new converts to his concept of justice. The times have never been more ready for his kind of steel nerves and defiantly aggressive defense. He who dares, wins.

Certainly the trigger-happy terrorists of Turkey and the Middle East in Bolan's new adventure will join the millions of "Bolan Watchers" who acknowledge *the Bolan effect*—the explosive, skin-shredding effect that his very specialized brand of warfare has on even the most prepared enemy.

There is only one Mack Bolan—and he is back at last!

---

Watch for *Double Crossfire*, Executioner #40, wherever paperback books are sold—in January, 1982.